- A CHANCE PURDUE MYSTERY -

ROSS H. SPENCER

DIVERSIONBOOKS

Also by Ross H. Spencer

Kirby's Last Circus
Death Wore Gloves

The Chance Purdue Series
The Dada Caper
The Reggis Arms Caper
The Abu Wahab Caper
The Radish River Caper

The Lacey Lockington Series
The Fifth Script
The Devereaux File
The Fedorovich File

Diversion Books
A Division of Diversion Publishing Corp.
443 Park Avenue South, Suite 1008
New York, New York 10016
www.DiversionBooks.com

For more information, email info@diversionbooks.com

First Diversion Books edition March 2015.
Print ISBN: 978-1-62681-963-4
eBook ISBN: 978-1-62681-652-7

This book is dedicated to my daughter Dawn,
the apple of mine fading eye.

…Somebody said that it couldn't be done…But I gallantly took up the fight…I gave it my best…and I'm here to attest that the bastard what said that was right…

Monroe D. Underwood

1

...fog is like marriage...getting into it is easy...

Monroe D. Underwood

A rolling barrage of June fog churned westward from Lake Michigan.

The Belmont Avenue traffic light glowed feeble emerald and the Old Washensachs sign in Wallace's window was barely visible as I drove south on Kimball.

I snailed the Olds through the gray murk and into the little parking lot behind Wallace's tavern.

I went in the back way.

Wallace said that Zizzenfrass guy called a couple minutes ago.

I said well I happen to have exactly what he's looking for.

I shoved a dollar bill at Wallace and got some telephone change.

I called Zizzenfrass.

I said can you talk freely?

Zizzenfrass said oh yes the cat's away.

He said as you know of course.

I said certainly but tell me do you have another operative watching your wife?

Zizzenfrass said oh no Purdue just you.

He said have you encountered some sort of difficulty?

I said let me take it from scratch.

I said your wife left the house at eight sharp.

I said she's a lovely young lady by the way.

Zizzenfrass chuckled a man-to-man chuckle.

He said well Purdue you see.

I said she drove directly to an apartment building in the sixty hundred block of North Kyle Boulevard.

Zizzenfrass said but Purdue.

I said she entered a garden apartment belonging to an R. Johannsen.

Zizzenfrass said Purdue as a matter of fact.

I said Mr. Zizzenfrass I have good reason to believe that a tall bony woman with a big nose is tailing your wife.

Zizzenfrass didn't say anything.

I said I talked to this tall bony woman and I got the distinct impression she is acquainted with you.

Zizzenfrass didn't say anything.

I said Mr. Zizzenfrass?

Zizzenfrass still didn't say anything.

I said Mr. Zizzenfrass are you there?

Zizzenfrass said big nose did you say?

I said oh boy.

I said like a goddam prize zucchini squash.

Zizzenfrass didn't say anything.

I said Mr. Zizzenfrass?

Zizzenfrass said Purdue why were you talking to this woman?

I said well it was sort of unavoidable.

I said she drove into the rear end of my automobile.

Zizzenfrass said how did the conversation go?

I said not too well.

I said she told me that I was a menace on the highways of America.

I said I explained that I wasn't on the highways of America.

I said I explained that I was parked in the lot of an apartment building.

Zizzenfrass said parked?

I said for two minutes.

Zizzenfrass said shall we get right to the part where I was mentioned?

I said she just asked why I was following Zizzenfrass's five-dollar whore.

Zizzenfrass made a strange gargling sound.

He said and what was your response?

I said oh I was very low key.

I said I simply pointed out that appearances are often deceiving and that Mrs. Zizzenfrass might very well be in there selling subscriptions to the *Lutheran Journal*.

I said I mentioned that the five-dollar whore is a thing of the past and that Mrs. Zizzenfrass was probably getting fifty if she was getting a dime.

I said I also told her that we should always say call girl not whore.

Zizzenfrass's voice downshifted into monotone.

Like when you tell the warden you have no final words.

He said Purdue how the hell did you ever get into the field of private investigation?

He said you have followed a call girl named Ruth

Johannsen from my home to her residence at 6030 North Kyle Boulevard.

He said my wife is supposedly in Vermont visiting a sick relative.

He said however my wife does not happen to be in Vermont visiting a sick relative.

He said my wife happens to be in our driveway getting out of her car.

He said there's a brand-new dent in the right front fender by the way.

He said and just look at that nose.

He said like a goddam prize zucchini squash.

I heard a door open.

I heard Zizzenfrass say hello Ophelia my dear.

I heard a sharp spanging sound.

I heard a heavy thump.

I heard Zizzenfrass gasp Purdue you're fired.

I shrugged.

I hung up.

2

> ...oncet I knowed a mayor what got lost in a fog
> and ended up in Congress...
>
> *Monroe D. Underwood*

The fog was a solid gray wall beyond the steady blue neon glow of Wallace's Old Washensachs beer sign.

The traffic signals at Belmont and Kimball had been swallowed.

Headlights groped yellowly through the tentacled night and sirens wailed like lost souls.

There was plenty of atmosphere but it was worthless.

Foggy nights don't matter much anymore.

It used to be you couldn't have a foggy night without a whole bunch of vampires and werewolves piling out of old castles and caves and starting a class AAA diarrhea epidemic.

In those days a private detective couldn't beat the customers off with a tire iron.

But that had been then and now it was now and now I

had nothing better to do than sit in Wallace's tavern and wait for Betsy to call and tell me to come home.

I lit an S-shaped Camel and listened to the jukebox play *Alte Kameraden.*

Wallace parked a bottle of Old Washensachs in front of me.

He said this one's on the house.

I said I just blew the Zizzenfrass case.

Wallace said well there ain't nobody never gonna accuse you of being inconsistent.

I shrugged.

Wallace said you're a lead-pipe cinch to make the Private Detective Hall of Fame.

I said I didn't know they had one.

Wallace said they don't but you ain't through yet.

I said don't bet on it.

Wallace said well I don't know about you but I am going to sell this roach ranch and go to Antarctica where I will run for mayor.

Old Dad Underwood said if you go to Antarctica you gonna be running for something besides mayor.

He said they already got a mayor.

Wallace said who?

Old Dad Underwood said a ten-foot-tall polar bear that's who.

He said I read all about him in *Better Homes and Gardens.*

The phone rang.

Wallace answered it and blushed and handed it to me.

Betsy's voice was brittle.

She said Chance just what did we sell the tavern back to Wallace for?

I said I think it was for five grand more than we paid

him for it.

Betsy made an impatient clicking sound.

She said Chance I know that.

She said what I meant was we might as well have kept it if you're going to take up residence there.

I said Betsy we couldn't have kept it.

I said the beer cooler was clanking.

I said anyway this is my office now.

Betsy said oh yes I saw your sign over the third booth.

I said well you got to admit the rent ain't bad.

Betsy said who did that sign?

I said Old Dad Underwood.

Betsy said well tell him there's no z in investigations.

I said that's not a z.

I said he just got his s backwards.

Betsy said I'll just leave that one alone thank you.

I said cheer up kiddo.

I said I should get a client any minute now.

I said it's a foggy night.

The line went dead.

3

> ...patriotism is same as the flu...everybody comes down with it but most manages to recover...
>
> *Monroe D. Underwood*

I lit an L-shaped Camel and hunched over my bottle of Old Washensachs.

I watched the fog billow by.

I said Wallace how did that Decoration Day party turn out?

Wallace turned slowly.

He said my God you don't remember?

I shrugged.

I said well not exactly.

Wallace said oh it was a darb.

He said you were at your patriotic peak.

He said you coldcocked a guy during the singing of "America the Beautiful."

I said you mean the smart sonofabitch who was singing *ach schon auf geraumig horizant* or some goddam thing?

Wallace said Chance the poor bastard was doing his best.

He said he was a visitor from Germany.

I said I see.

Wallace said after that you sang "My Buddy" and you recited "Barbara Frietchie" and while you were doing the manual of arms with a broom you busted a fifth of Sunnybrook and Brightside Nelson's false teeth.

He said Brightside Nelson bit you on the ankle.

I said well that just may explain that cracked upper plate I found in my shoe.

I said what was Brightside Nelson so pissed off about?

Wallace said it was his fifth of Sunnybrook.

I shrugged.

Wallace said you may have a client.

He said a guy just took a seat in your office.

4

...baseball is only a game but you ain't never gonna get nobody to believe that...

Monroe D. Underwood

He sat in the third booth with his pearl-gray fedora pushed to the back of his head.

He was a sturdily built man with a pockmarked face and reptilian eyes and a mouth like a saber slash.

His black shirt was wrinkled and his white necktie was undone and his powder-blue suit was wilted.

He looked up at me and said hey kid thatta sonnabitcha fog justa like soup out there.

I sat across from Cool Lips Chericola.

Cool Lips Chericola was Chicago's Mafia boss.

I said well there never was much I could do about fog.

I said sir.

Chericola put a match to a nine-dollar Havana cigar the size of a Genoa salami.

In a moment the cigar smoke was thicker than the fog.

I said I heard the feds had you over a barrel for shoplifting in a government arsenal.

Chericola flashed a smoke-shrouded Cheshire cat grin.

He said hey kid you gotta know the righta peoples.

He said you know the righta peoples is everything coming uppa roses.

I shrugged.

I said you'll never prove it by me.

Chericola said hey kid lasta time seeing you is atta Reggis Arms Hotel.

I said yeah Pearl Harbor Day.

Chericola said who that sharpa broad you hanga round with then?

I shrugged.

I said she was some sort of detective.

I said we were looking for somebody who never got there.

Chericola said where she now?

I shrugged.

I fired up a J-shaped Camel.

I blew my smoke at Chericola's smoke.

Like a guy with a carbine shooting it out with two battleships and a heavy cruiser.

I said why?

Chericola said is gotta gooda job for her.

He said checka up onna business venture.

I said you got anything against her?

Chericola threw back his head and laughed.

He said hey kid amma like thatta broad.

He said she's hate them Communistics justa like me.

I shrugged.

I said I'm afraid I can't tell you anything.

Chericola chuckled through a dragon-style cloud of cigar smoke.

He said thattsa my boy.

He said is gooda man whatta sticka by his friends.

He said hey kid her name Brandy Alexander and she's own Confidential Investigations inna Loop.

He said she's already tooka job and she's recommenda you for reala nice assignment I'm givva you.

I said no thanks.

I said you see I got this allergy to getting stuffed into Pontiac trunks.

I said the same allergy Stiff Socks Castellano probably had.

Chericola said hey kid you patriotic no?

I shrugged.

I said I've had my moments.

Chericola said you know when Stiffa Socksa Castellano going all wrong?

I shrugged.

I said yeah when he got stuffed into that Pontiac trunk.

Chericola shook his head sadly.

He leaned through the smoke.

He lowered his voice.

He said hey kid Stiffa Socksa Castellano is forgetta words to "America the Beautiful."

I said well hell that's different.

I said you should have stuffed the sonofabitch into a Toyota glove compartment.

Chericola said thattsa my boy.

He said hey kid you liking baseball?

I shrugged.

I said it beats Russian roulette.

Chericola said you ever playa baseball?

I said sure I pitched American Legion ball until I hit our manager in the mouth during batting practice.

Chericola sniffed disdainfully.

He said is serva him right.

He said batta practice for players notta managers.

I shrugged.

I said well this particular manager was eating a candy bar in the dugout at the time.

I said I think it was a wild pitch.

Chericola said hey kid he's forgetta firsta rule inna game.

He said keepa eye onna goddam ball.

I said how does baseball fit into the picture?

Chericola blew smoke like an overdue Twentieth Century Limited.

He said amma buy minor league baseball team inna southern Illinois.

I said how come you went clear to southern Illinois?

I said you could have got one right here in Chicago.

Chericola said amma wanta you go down looka over team.

He said amma wanta report onna whole operation.

He said how sixxa hundred?

I said per month?

Chericola frowned.

He said hey kid you talking to not no cheapaskate.

He said per day.

I said I'm can'ta leave forra tenna minutes.

Chericola shrugged.

5

> ...never knowed nobody what wasn't a stranger firstest time I met 'em...
>
> *Monroe D. Underwood*

The fog was lifting and the cigar smoke was gone.

Wallace said who was that mean-looking gorilla?

I shrugged.

I said just a guy who gave me a job in some burg called Stranger City.

Wallace said well he had a Cadillac about forty feet long.

He said with a goddam chauffeur yet.

I said Wallace where the hell is Stranger City?

Wallace gave me a look of disbelief.

He said Chance do you mean to sit there and tell me you never heard of Stranger City?

I said why hell yes I mean to sit here and tell you I never heard of Stranger City.

I said what's so goddam unusual about never hearing of

a place nobody ever heard of?

Wallace said why a long time ago Stranger City was real big news.

I said so was Halley's comet.

Wallace said I got the whole Stranger City story out of some book.

Old Dad Underwood said what was the name of it?

Wallace folded his arms across his chest.

He glared at Old Dad Underwood.

He said the name of it was *The Whole Stranger City Story.*

Old Dad Underwood said how many crayons you use up?

I said tell me what happened in Stranger City for Christ's sake.

Wallace said well there was a dozen bad guys blowed in and they was going to take over the town only this here stranger showed up and wiped 'em out.

Old Dad Underwood said what was he packing some kind of death-ray?

Wallace said he wasn't packing nothing but a pair of six-guns.

Old Dad Underwood said what color?

Wallace said black.

Old Dad Underwood said you colored 'em wrong.

He said they is blue.

I said on with the story.

Wallace said well he kilt twelve guys with twelve shots.

Old Dad Underwood said didn't nobody notice if he was riding a white horse?

Wallace said didn't nobody notice much of anything.

He said he was a stranger.

He said that's why they call it Stranger City.

He said you can figger that out can't you?

Old Dad Underwood said what did they call it before they called it Stranger City?

Wallace said Lilacville.

He said they had a whole mess of them yellow flowers all over.

Old Dad Underwood said lilacs ain't yellow.

Wallace said well they was yellow when I got through.

Old Dad Underwood said I like Lilacville better.

Wallace put his hands on his hips.

He said just how many drinks you had?

Old Dad Underwood said I never count drinks.

He said I work it with percentages.

He said like just now I am maybe sixty-two percent through give or take a few nightcaps.

Wallace said well maybe you would be sixty-two percent through if you was over at Spud's place but in Wallace's tavern you are one hunnert percent through and there ain't gonna be no nightcaps.

I said good God will you finish the story?

Wallace said this here stranger got kilt in the shoot-out but he saved Stranger City and nobody never found out who he was.

Old Dad Underwood said Jesus Christ.

Wallace shook his head.

He said he didn't have no beard.

6

> ...Halley's comet is something what is a million years old and comes around scaring people half to death...exactly like my mother-in-law...
>
> *Monroe D. Underwood*

Betsy brought me an ice-cold bottle of Old Washensachs.

She sat close beside me on the couch.

She said honey weren't you working for a Reginald Zizzenfrass recently?

I shrugged.

I said more or less.

I said it all depends on how you look at it.

Betsy said the late news mentioned that an Ophelia Zizzenfrass shot a Reginald Zizzenfrass in the foot.

I shrugged.

I said there are probably a hundred million Reginald Zizzenfrasses.

Betsy said tell me about your Stranger City job.

She said in the first place I've never even heard of Stranger City.

I said why a long time ago Stranger City was real big news.

Betsy said so was Halley's comet.

I said well my client bought a minor league baseball team down there.

Betsy said why did he go to Stranger City?

She said he could have bought one right here in Chicago.

I said they're scheduled to practice on Saturday and Sunday and open their season on Monday.

I said all I have to do is look the situation over and send my client a report.

Betsy said how long will it take?

I said I'll leave Friday morning and get back next week.

Betsy said it sounds okay and that may be precisely what's wrong with it.

She stared at the floor.

When she looked up there were tears in her big pale blue eyes.

She said lover I'm going to miss you.

I shrugged.

I took Cool Lips Chericola's advance one-thousand-dollar bill from my pocket.

I inserted it in Betsy's gorgeous cleavage.

I said there's a couple more where that one came from.

I said it'll be the first damn dollar I've earned since I blew the Williams case.

Betsy said Chance I haven't been hounding you for money.

She said I keep calling you because I miss your company.

I said I know that.

I said it's just that a guy has to get out and scare up a

buck every so often.

Betsy said scaring up a buck is perfectly okay.

She said but you scared up a doe at the Reggis Arms.

I said aw come on Betsy don't you know me better than that?

Betsy said huh-uh.

She squeezed my leg.

She said just what am I supposed to do for this one-thousand-dollar bill?

I shrugged.

I said anything that strikes your fancy.

Betsy said you know what strikes my fancy.

I said are you talking about the same thing that always strikes your fancy?

Betsy said Chance do you honestly believe I'm a sex maniac?

I shrugged.

I said aren't you?

Betsy smiled sweetly.

She was the most beautiful blonde on the face of Planet Earth.

She said sweetheart you'd better believe it.

She said but how did you know?

I said I'm a detective.

Betsy stood and took my hand.

She said come with me.

She said I have a red-hot case that requires your immediate attention.

7

> ...religion is just like a venereal disease...you catch it and then you give it to somebody else and you have a fine time in both cases...
>
> *Monroe D. Underwood*

Friday started out all wrong.

The alarm went off.

Then Betsy drove me to the Happy Trails bus depot at Randolph and State.

In typical Betsy Purdue fashion.

With her foot in the carburetor.

I said slow down.

In typical Chance Purdue fashion.

With my heart in my mouth.

Betsy said Chance we aren't in a funeral procession you know.

I said no but we'll be in one on Monday if you don't slow down.

Betsy said do you want to drive?

I said Betsy for Christ's sake shut up and watch out for that goddam big truck.

Betsy said I see it I see it.

I said well my God you ought to see it.

I said we're only two feet behind it.

Betsy said oh that goddam big truck.

She said I thought you meant the goddam big truck that's only two feet behind us.

Somewhere between a cold sweat and Randolph Street Betsy gave me a stern lecture on the dangers of sleeping with strange women in strange towns.

She mentioned gonorrhea and syphilis.

She brought up the horrors of Medusa's Revenge.

I said I never heard of Medusa's Revenge.

Betsy shuddered.

She said oh let's not even talk about it.

I said okay.

8

> ...oncet I knowed a whorehouse madam what went straight to hell...she cheated on her church tithe...
>
> *Monroe D. Underwood*

It was seven-thirty when I stumbled up to the ticket window.

The clerk said yes sir?

I said round-trip to Stranger City.

The clerk said you could still change your mind.

He said Heppner Oregon is a nice town.

He said why not Laurel Mississippi?

I said why not Stranger City like I asked for in the first place?

The clerk said because you'll be riding the Double Eagle Line.

I said is the Double Eagle Line the best way to get there?

The clerk said it ain't the best way but it's the only way.

He handed me a big piece of cardboard that looked like it had been clipped from a milk carton.

I looked it over.

I said this is a one-way ticket.

The clerk said the Double Eagle Line don't sell no round-trip tickets.

I said why is that?

The clerk said you'll find out why is that.

I said how long to get there?

The clerk said five to ten hours if everything goes right.

He said gate three you daredevil.

I grabbed my suitcase and barged out of gate three.

When I saw what was out there I damn near barged back into the terminal.

My bus was an ancient black Reo.

It was idling and it shook like it had malaria.

Great threatening bluish-white exhaust puffs spurted from the belly of the relic.

The fabric of the huge tires was visible and rubber remnants hung in limp strips like from a cat-o'-nine-tails.

The right-hand side of the apparition bore a giant painting of two birds in flight.

The lead bird clutched a dozen ecstatically smiling travelers.

I noted that the male passengers in the picture wore raccoon coats.

The second bird carried several pieces of luggage most of which resembled pirate chests.

I got a C-shaped Camel going and walked to the front of the bus.

I gulped tobacco smoke and carbon monoxide in equal quantities.

I saw no destination sign.

Through the cobwebbed windshield I watched the driver rise to turn a little crank.

White print flashed unreadably by until the numbers

87-1 were frozen in place.

I shrugged.

I crossed my fingers and swung aboard.

The driver was a skinny kid with watery blue eyes and a straggly yellow moustache.

He wore a World War I aviator's helmet complete with goggles and long white scarf.

He caught me staring at his medal.

He said Blue Max.

I nodded.

Matter-of-factly I hoped.

I said tell me about the numbers on the front of this scrap pile.

The driver tightened his chin strap and adjusted his goggles.

He said them's the odds.

He said I was sort of hoping they might be the number of the bus.

The driver said don't be silly.

He said this is the only bus we got.

I sat behind a fat old lady with bright orange hair.

She was wrestling a quart bottle of pills.

I reached over and helped her open it.

She gave me a ghastly smile.

She said dearie have you ridden the Double Eagle Line before?

I said no ma'am I think I would have remembered.

She said here dearie have some tranquilizers.

She gave me a handful.

They were ornery-looking little green bastards.

The driver looked back and gave us a thumbs-up sign.

We blasted out of the depot in a vast cloud of steam and smoke.

At the first traffic light a priest opened a window and jumped.

He called for his suitcase and I threw it to him.

He smiled his gratitude and made some motions with his hands.

I said it was nice of him to give us a blessing.

The fat old lady said dearie I'm Seventh Day Adventist but I know the last rites when I see 'em.

We ripped the stop sign from a school bus and we ran a gasoline tanker into a ditch and we put a squad car through a sign board.

I almost wished Betsy was driving.

We hit the expressway and the driver flogged his steaming steed to the outside and really got down to business.

The threadbare tires sizzled like frying bacon.

Telephone poles zipped past like fence pickets.

The fat old lady was mumbling something.

I caught the words cleft for me.

We dusted off a Corvette and an ambulance.

I noticed that the fat old lady's hair was snow white.

I tapped her gently on the shoulder.

I said beg pardon ma'am but your hair has turned white.

The fat old lady said I know it dearie my wig just flew off.

I said I'm sorry that priest bailed out.

I said he might have been useful.

The fat old lady said not really dearie.

She said I wouldn't have had time to confess all my sins.

She said I got to change buses in Putnam.

I said my gosh ma'am Putnam is two hundred miles from here.

The fat old lady said dearie I run a whorehouse in Kane Corners.

9

> …my mother-in-law spent five days in the Smithsonian Institute…took her four days to convince them she wasn't some kind of spaceship…
>
> *Monroe D. Underwood*

The Double Eagle Line anachronism took a sharp bend on two wheels.

It ran onto the shoulder long enough to wipe out a row of mailboxes.

It straightened out and plunged down a long shady hill like a four-wheeled avalanche.

I had the Blue Max business all figured out.

This maniac thought he was Baron Richthofen.

By God maybe he was.

The reincarnation theory had gained respectable support over the years.

At the bottom of the incline the Reo's engine sputtered into silence.

We coasted blissfully for a mile before groaning to a stop.

The driver hollered Stranger City.

I took my suitcase and went up front.

We were parked by a stand of white birches.

I looked in all directions.

I said where the hell is Stranger City?

The driver pointed through the fractured windshield.

He said take the first fork to the left and you're almost there.

I said just a minute Baron my ticket says Stranger City.

The driver spread his hands palms up.

He said sorry mister the bus is busted.

I said what's the trouble?

The driver said could be either the water pump or the transmission.

I said look Junior you just crank this heap up and take me to Stranger City.

The driver said impossible.

He said I got to make repairs.

He said we might be here for hours.

I said they ought to stick this monstrosity in the goddam Smithsonian Institution.

The driver shook his head.

He said the Smithsonian won't take it back.

I used a four-letter word and got off.

I hiked a quarter-mile to the fork and made the turn.

A moment later the bus buzzed down the main pike like a teed-off hornet.

I saw that there was no painting of birds on its lefthand side.

Just a huge black Maltese cross.

10

> ...if all the zeroes was stacked up in one place you'd sure have one hell of a pile of nothing...
>
> *Monroe D. Underwood*

The dusty road wandered aimlessly through thistle and barbed bushes and gnarled trees.

The sky was cobalt blue and the afternoon sun was merciless and you could have hacked the silence with a cleaver.

I took off my sports coat and stuffed it through my suitcase handle.

I unbuttoned my collar and started walking.

I thought of Blind Johnny Jackson the old black singer on Adams Street and his "Dusty Road Blues."

The saddest baddest low-down blues this poor boy ever knowed was them blues he got on a dusty road.

Or something like that.

Well look out Stranger City.

Out of the dust here comes Chance Purdue private

detective par excellence.

The man whose life looks like a White Sox box score.

Zeroes.

Except in the errors column.

And Betsy.

There was Betsy.

Betsy was no zero.

I missed her.

11

> ...oncet I knowed a feller what said he was most anxious to assume responsibility...last I heard of him he had hisself a widow and her six kids and her eighty-five thousand dollar mortgage...reckon that ought to hold him for a while...
>
> *Monroe D. Underwood*

The dusty road approached Stranger City cautiously.

It employed any number of last-minute zigs and zags.

An obvious delaying action that I understood.

Responsibility lay ahead.

Now it slipped unobtrusively into the little town from the north.

Or what seemed like the north.

An hour of tracing its moody meanderings had left me directionless.

Suddenly it became Stranger Avenue.

It remained unpaved and rutted and dusty but for

five halfhearted blocks it was Stranger City's principal thoroughfare.

It ran almost straight as it conformed reluctantly to its brief role of importance.

Then it chucked all obligations to become gloriously free.

Again it was a road for a boy with a straw hat and a cane fishing pole.

It wound its happily erratic way into the blue distance.

I watched it depart with a vague sadness.

We had been friends for a time.

12

…you show me a park-bench philosopher and I'll show you a man what got splinters in his ass…

Monroe D. Underwood

Stranger City must have been the lilac capital of Illinois.

It was drenched in the scent.

The population might have approached two thousand if you counted stray dogs and the goat tethered in the first yard I passed.

It had an eight-lane bowling house and a single-pump gas station and a grocery store with a placard in its window.

DOCTOR JAKE BURNHAM ENTRANCE IN REAR.

I saw a tiny red-brick schoolhouse and a couple of restaurants and a diner painted purple.

There was a small bank and a library and a ramshackle frame hotel and a shanty the size of a double-garage that had an overhanging sign saying SHURFF.

Out of the shanty came an old bandy-legged man who

wore a white Stetson and a plaid shirt.

The cuffs of his khaki pants were stuffed into short black western-style boots.

He walked with a jauntiness that belied his age.

He piled into a mint-condition blue Model A Ford with a silver star on its door.

The rumble seat had been slightly modified to accommodate a boxlike object shielded from weather by a gaudy red and yellow canopy.

The old man started the engine and the strains of a barrel organ drifted from the rear of the automobile as it purred away into the golden afternoon.

I couldn't place the song.

It was a dreamily sweet little ditty yet there was infinite melancholy in it.

I came to a grassy park across the street from the hotel and I dropped my suitcase and sat on a bench.

I poured a pint of pebbles out of each shoe and a quart of dust out of each sock.

I wiggled my toes in the soft green grass.

During the time it required to smoke a pair of squashed Camels a dilapidated pickup truck struggled by and a couple of youngsters got ice cream cones at the grocery store.

The kid with the strawberry cone had freckles.

The vintage vehicle returned with its haunting tune.

The pristine notes spanned an ocean of time and tumult.

I watched the little blue car do a U-turn in the dusty street and stop under the sign that said SHURFF.

The old man killed the engine and the music died away.

I tried to recall a school-days poem.

Something about a barrel organ in lilac time.

I stuffed my socks into a pocket and slipped into my shoes and crossed the street.

I was the oldest man on earth.

13

> ...the Bible is a book what said just about everything was a sin...when the collection plates started coming back empty the churches read the Bible again...they suddenly discovered that just about everything was perfeckly permissible... makes a man stop and wonder don't it?...
>
> *Monroe D. Underwood*

The interior of the Stranger City Hotel was dim and damp.

It would have blown an antique collector's mind.

The balding carpeting featured little flying cupids.

Thick sun-ravaged red velvet draperies cascaded over the windows.

Time-yellowed wallpaper depicted a Bavarian boar hunt in which the hounds looked exactly like the boars.

There was a morris chair and a sagging davenport with cracked leather and a great many inhospitable highbacked rocking chairs.

There were a half-dozen chipped mahogany tables and a Victrola and floor lamps with long-tasseled shades and several fat brass spittoons.

I walked to the desk.

The desk clerk was a fidgety little perspiring guy.

Behind his thick-lensed spectacles his amber eyes gleamed like harbor lights.

I didn't have to catch his attention.

He had watched me like a hungry hawk.

I said Chance Purdue.

The desk clerk nodded and handed me a huge key.

It looked like it would have unlocked the private vault of King Nebuchadnezzar.

I signed the register and studied the faded reproduction of "Curfew Shall Not Ring Tonight" hanging lopsidedly on the back wall of the office.

I said I haven't seen one like that in a long time.

The desk clerk pointed to a painting that decorated one side of his alcove.

He said there's one I bet you ain't never seen.

He said that's by Horatio Brayfuss and it's a original.

I didn't know who Horatio Brayfuss was but the painting was just about as original as they come.

It was crudely done and it didn't leave much to the imagination.

It showed a tall man clad in black crouched menacingly in a frontier-type saloon.

His smoking revolvers weren't a great deal larger than 105mm howitzers.

At his feet sprawled several villainous-looking characters.

To have remarked that they were dead would have been

the understatement of the century.

Their eyeballs were rolled up into their heads and torrents of blood gushed through the sawdust of the barroom floor.

There was a halo hovering just above the crown of the tall man's black hat.

It was faint but clearly discernible.

The desk clerk's amber eyes searched my face.

He said that's The Stranger.

He said The Stranger killed a dozen guys to save this town.

He gestured with his thumb through a door to my left.

He said it happened right there in the lounge.

He said hey you can talk about your heroes but I'll take The Stranger any old time.

He said God rest his soul.

He said that's why they call us Stranger City.

I shrugged.

I said I notice that Stranger City has a musical squad car.

The desk clerk said yeah the shurff makes a buck or two with that barrel organ.

He said ice cream socials and the like.

He said it runs off a compressor and he got the whole shooting match wired to the ignition.

He said can't you just see the old bastard chasing a bunch of crooks with his goddam barrel organ blasting out that honky-tonk tune?

I shrugged.

I said what's its name?

The desk clerk frowned.

He said even the shurff don't know.

He said did the shurff arrest you yet?

I said no will he?

The desk clerk said oh sure he'll get you on suspicion of some goddam thing or other.

He said you'll have to post bond.

He said bond is usually a fifth of whiskey but you look like a pint case to me.

He said couple days ago the shurff arrested a preacher on suspicion of being a smuggler.

I said smuggling what?

The desk clerk said Bibles into public schools.

I said good God that's a serious charge these days.

The desk clerk said hey they lynched a preacher over in Jericho Ridge.

I shrugged.

I said well a town without a lynching is no town at all.

The desk clerk said that's exactly what the boys figgered.

He said they boiled it down to where it was either the preacher or the taxidermist.

He said they lynched the preacher on account of they needed the taxidermist to stuff him.

He said they got that preacher smack-dab in the middle of the religious section in the Jericho Ridge library.

He said frocked coat and all.

I shrugged.

I said well look what I really had in mind was locating a man named Rube Mountainstill who's the manager of your new ball team.

The desk clerk said that's Mountainstill over in the morris chair.

He said he hiked in here yesterday after the Double Eagle Line bus broke down.

He said the shurff arrested him soon as he seen him.

He said suspicion of being a Martian secret agent.

I grinned.

I said I'll bet Mountainstill was sore.

The desk clerk said no he just throwed up his hands and come clean.

He said he admitted his real name was Gorm and he owned up to being over three million years old.

He said they talked for better than a hour.

He said before they got done the shurff give Mountainstill a half-gallon of Old Anchor Chain.

He said mighty fine six-month-old stuff.

14

...oncet I knowed a man what studied trigonometry till he found out nobody could speak it...

Monroe D. Underwood

Rube Mountainstill was a long lean leathery man with a full head of silvery hair.

He was at the high-tide of his sixties and he had soft brown understanding eyes and a slim high-bridge nose and a thin-lipped mouth and a jaw that said sorry but that's the way it is.

He was a dead ringer for that uncle you didn't meet until you were over thirty.

He was munching the tattered stub of a dead cigar and reading a paperback copy of *The Decline and Fall of Just About Everything.*

I said Mr. Mountainstill I'm Chance Purdue from Chicago.

Rube looked up.

He said last feller what called me mister picked my pocket.

He straightened in the morris chair and tossed his book

into a wastebasket.

He said I never read such optimistic sugarcoated drivel in all my born days.

His voice was gentle but his handshake was like a vise.

He said you're Chericola's guy.

I shrugged.

I said just for a few days.

Rube glanced at a huge horse-faced man who slept open-mouthed on the davenport.

He said I'd introduce you to Moose Edwards but he'd just forget who you are anyway.

I said Rube do you own a very large black German shepherd dog?

Rube said well let's just say we is associates.

He said just who owns who ain't been established yet.

I said what do you call him?

Rube said oh any number of things.

He said Count Frazzlewitz usually but it depends on what he happens to be up to.

I said well right about now he happens to be up to chewing a front leg off of that morris chair.

Rube sighed.

He said well son in a town like this a body just got to amuse hisself best way he can.

He said if my teeth was better I'd be working on a back leg.

Rube stood up.

He was stooped but he stood tall in his loose-fitting brown suit.

I said I just got in here yesterday.

I said what are you in a position to tell me?

Rube said I am in a position to tell you there are a great

many places I would much rather be.

He said among these are Sodom and Gomorrah and Jasper Texas.

He led the way into the lounge.

It was a sparsely furnished long low room of age-darkened wood.

There was a regulator clock on one wall and on another was a rough wooden sign that said THE STRANGER 12—BAD GUYS 1.

Over the cash register I saw a painting of a blonde smiling man.

He wore a white hat above which floated a tiny golden halo.

Rube and I sat on wobbly wooden stools and we ordered bourbon and water.

The bartender was a short burly man with a beet-red face and glittering gray eyes.

He said are you gentlemen going to the fifteenth annual Stranger City Baseball Ball on Sunday night?

Rube said Sunday night?

I said fifteenth?

The bartender said yep and next year will be our sixteenth.

Rube said trigonometry always throwed me.

I said but this is the first year you've had a ball team.

The bartender said we been holding baseball balls just in case we ever got one.

I said I see.

Rube said I don't.

He said keep talking and maybe it will come to me.

I pointed to the painting above the old NCR 410.

I said who's that?

The bartender said that's The Stranger.

He said Horatio Brayfuss painted that.

I said how many Strangers were there?

The bartender said one was all we needed.

I said but this Stranger is wearing a white hat and the one in the office is wearing a black hat.

The bartender said well Horatio Brayfuss is the only one what seen him and Brayfuss painted both pictures and there just ain't nobody argues with Horatio Brayfuss.

Rube ordered another round and his voice dropped to super-secret level.

He said say when you was coming down here did you happen to come acrost a gray-haired woman what is about five foot tall and goes maybe a hunnert pounds providing she is carrying a set of Funkin Wagner's encyclopedias?

I shrugged.

I said Rube there must be lots of women like that.

Rube shook his head.

Emphatically.

He said oh no there ain't.

He said this woman got violet eyes and she speaks Chinese with a Polish accent and on her left arm she got a tattoo what says Tillie Loves Rube.

I shrugged.

I said tell me about the tattoo.

Rube said well it's blue and red and it got crossed American flags and there is this great big hairy bird sitting betwixt the flagpoles and in his beak he got this banner what says Tillie Loves Rube.

He said it cost Tillie twenny dollars back in the thirties and it got to be worth a fortune now.

He said damn pity she can't sell it.

I shrugged.

I said Rube I haven't seen her.

Rube grinned.

He said well by golly maybe I got it done.

He said maybe I have escaped from Tillie Zilch.

He drained his glass and waved for refills.

He said thirty-nine years.

His voice trailed off to a whisper and he brushed away a tear.

He said it took me thirty-nine years.

15

> ...finding a woman in your hotel room is like finding a nine hunnert dollar bill in your wallet...all of a sudden you got yourself one helluva good chance to get in a whole heap of trouble...
>
> *Monroe D. Underwood*

Room 204 was stuffy.

I left the door open and raised both windows.

The curtains swelled in the late afternoon breeze and the sweetness of lilacs floated into the room.

I sat on the bed and looked around.

At one time the walls might have been blue.

They also might have been green.

Now the paint was blistered and peeling and they resembled miniature battlefields.

There was a hole in the bedspread.

There was a hole in the throw rug.

I lifted one end of it and found a hole in the carpeting.

There was a gash in the shade of the lamp on the splintered nightstand.

The Gideon Bible was dog-eared.

I opened it to its yellow silk marker and saw that Genesis 23:4 had been snipped out.

I placed a cracked ashtray beside me and lit a wilted Camel.

I dropped the paper match into the ashtray and watched it curl grayly.

Like a man's dreams.

I heard a car door slam.

I walked to the window and saw a supercharged silvergray Porsche parked in front of the hotel.

Its flowing lines were in violent disagreement with the straight up and down feel of Stranger City.

A tall gaunt white-haired man sat on the park bench I had occupied earlier.

He was very old.

He wore an ill-fitting dark blue suit with an open-collared tan shirt and his buckthorn cane rested between his legs.

The lilac fragrance was stronger now.

Much stronger.

Too goddam strong.

I spun around.

The most beautiful brunette on the face of Planet Earth stood very close to me.

Her dark wavy hair cascaded to her shoulders.

Her liquid brown eyes sparkled.

Her full lips smiled a wonderfully warm smile.

She said hello Purdue.

I shrugged.

I said hello Brandy.

Brandy shook her head in vexed fashion.

Like you do when you can't find your car keys.

She said Purdue I had made up my mind that I'd never see you again.

She said but when the opportunity presented itself I just couldn't stand my ground.

She said you understand.

I shrugged.

I said how did you work it?

Brandy said Chericola came to my agency and offered me a perfectly legitimate job.

She said I realized that I could tie it in with something else and I accepted on the condition that you be included.

She said it's that simple.

I said does Chericola know you busted up his December operation?

Brandy winked at me.

She said no that's privileged information.

She said Chericola likes me because I hate Communism.

I said how's your agency doing?

Brandy said far better than I expected.

She said any more questions?

I shrugged.

I said just one.

I said have you ever gotten around to wearing half-slips?

Brandy turned and closed the door.

She hooked the night chain.

She slipped into my arms.

Her lilac perfume was heady and her soft perfect lips

were eager and her liquid brown eyes were turbulent.

She said find out for yourself Purdue.

Brandy Alexander still wasn't wearing half-slips.

16

> …oncet I knowed a man what joined the CIA and blowed up the White House…that Communist Infiltration Association don't mess around…
>
> *Monroe D. Underwood*

It was early evening and we shared the cracked ashtray.

Brandy's cigarette glowed ruby in the dim little room.

She said do you miss Betsy?

I said sure but not like I did a few hours ago.

Brandy said Purdue you should have been a diplomat.

She kissed me gently.

She said do you know how wonderful this is?

I shrugged.

I said I think I'm beginning to get the idea.

Brandy said since last December I've done nothing but dream.

I said about what?

Brandy said about last December of course.

I said what's the score down here?

Brandy said your end of the deal is a snap.

She said no cloak-and-dagger malarkey.

She said just work up some sort of comprehensive report on the baseball team and its gate potential.

I said what will you be doing?

Brandy said I'll be using the baseball thing as a cover while I work on a matter for the CIA.

I said does Chericola know you'll be going two ways?

Brandy said what Chericola doesn't know won't hurt him a bit.

I said I thought you had quit the CIA.

Brandy said Purdue nobody quits the CIA.

She said not completely.

She said there's always that old alma mater loyalty.

She said gosh we have operatives that get around on canes.

I said after getting worked over in an alley?

Brandy said after getting old wise guy.

She said I have to run over to Raccoon Rapids this evening but I'll have time to trim your sails again.

I said forget it.

I said my main mast is down.

Brandy said I'll fix it.

She said I'm very good with main masts.

I shrugged.

17

> …Philadelphia is a place I allus wanted to see but some dirty bastard busted the Liberty Bell and they traded Mickey Cochrane to Detroit…
>
> *Monroe D. Underwood*

The Stranger City Diner may have been the very first railroad passenger car.

It was good to see the poor thing at rest.

It stood at the north end of town surrounded by neatly trimmed Japanese yews.

Its interior gleamed hospitably and an elderly man with a magnificent bristling white moustache was quick to pour a steaming cup of coffee from a battered pot half the size of a rain barrel.

Either the country air had meddled with my taste buds or it was the finest cup of coffee in history.

I nodded hello.

I said I'm Chance Purdue and I just got into town.

The guy with the moustache said well I'm Cemetery Carson and I just got arrested.

He said bond was a fifth of Foggy Mountain.

I said what was the charge?

Cemetery Carson said suspicion of cheating at cards.

I whistled.

I said do you?

Cemetery said well sure but I never play nothing but solitaire.

He said hell that's a two-way street.

He said I been cheated aplenty times playing solitaire.

I ordered a hot beef sandwich.

I said with the nearest railroad over forty miles from here how did they get this car to Stranger City?

Cemetery grinned a toothless grin.

He said wasn't much to it.

He said the big wind of 'sixteen blowed her in.

I washed that down with a swallow of coffee.

I said you had a wind that blew a goddam railroad car forty miles?

Cemetery said may of been lots farther than that.

He said nobody could read the printing on her.

I said obliterated?

Cemetery said huh?

I said why couldn't they read the printing?

Cemetery said it was in some foreign language.

I said strong wind.

Cemetery said ooo-eee.

He said wasn't a haystack left in seven counties.

I said why do they call you Cemetery?

Cemetery looked surprised.

He said because I own the Stranger City cemetery.

I winked at him.

I said a cemetery owner shouldn't be working in a diner.

I said he should be busy burying people.

Cemetery said shoot ain't nobody been buried in these parts since The Stranger blasted them twelve bastards.

He filled my coffee cup.

I said you must have a crematory.

Cemetery said sure but you drunk the first cup black.

I said well at least you buried The Stranger and the bad guys.

Cemetery said no I didn't.

He said immediately after it happened Horatio Brayfuss dug a hole for 'em over by the ball park.

He said few years later we put the baseball clubhouse right on top of 'em.

I shrugged.

I said it would seem The Stranger deserved better than that.

Cemetery said oh The Stranger ain't with that riffraff.

He said Brayfuss put him way up on Darby's Jump Off.

He said it's real nice up thataway.

He said The Stranger got a big monument and everything.

I said what's Darby's Jump Off?

Cemetery said it's a cliff a couple hunnert foot above the river.

He said long way down.

He said ooo-eee.

I said I suppose somebody named Darby jumped off.

Cemetery said nope Darby never jumped off but he was always threatening to.

He said drove everybody crazy.

He said it got so bad the city council give him a choice.

He said jump off or get throwed off.

He said actually Darby choked to death on a New York cherry ice cream cone.

He said in Philadelphia.

I didn't say anything.

Cemetery slid my hot beef sandwich down the counter.

He said you want a slice of raw onion?

I shrugged.

Cemetery dropped an onion cartwheel into my plate.

It splashed gravy on my shirt.

18

> ...oncet I knowed a widow what called in a piano tuner...claimed her bedsprings was squeaking out of key...they managed to get 'em adjusted...
>
> *Monroe D. Underwood*

The vast velvet sky was cloudless.

There were twenty million stars.

Approximately.

Not run-of-the-mill stars.

Big shiny ones.

I trudged along a dusty footpath under a great butteryellow moon.

I found the park bench.

I sat and lit a corkscrew Camel.

Somewhere in the night an out-of-tune piano was playing "Sweet Hour of Prayer."

I listened.

There were no other sounds.

I was up to my knees in yesterday.
I found moisture on my cheeks.
Dew.
Probably.

19

…whiskey is a terrible thing…it makes people act just like people…

Monroe D. Underwood

I sat on the park bench for nearly an hour.

The old piano knocked me out.

I heard "He Lifted Me Up" and "Brighten the Corner Where You Are" and "In the Garden" and a few I didn't recognize.

It was during "He Keeps Me Singing" that I realized my hotel room light had been turned on.

That would have been all right but Brandy's Porsche hadn't returned.

The only person in the hotel lobby was the desk clerk.

The only sound was his raspy snoring from the depths of the morris chair.

I climbed the stairs quietly and found my door open.

The shurff was sprawled on my bed.

He was reading my Gideon Bible.

He was a wiry little guy with snowy hair and laughing bright blue eyes.

He grinned disarmingly.

He said reckoned I ought to come by and shake hands and say howdy.

We shook hands and said howdy.

I said when do I get arrested?

The shurff said oh don't worry I'll git around to you.

He said first I got to think of something to arrest you on suspicion of.

I shrugged.

I said how about suspicion of bringing a fifth of Sunnybrook across the county line?

The shurff shook his head.

His expression was grave.

He said well now if you really done something turrbul like that bout the onliest way you could git out of it would be if I was to drink up the evvydence.

I took a bottle from my suitcase and handed it over.

The shurff hoisted it and said well now what could I maybe do for you?

I shrugged.

I said well for one thing you might fill me in on this Stranger yarn.

The shurff lit right into it.

He said well you see it was Fourth of July and the whole dang town was out to Ike Kelton's farm.

He said they had a big barbycue and when it come dark they shot off all them Roman candles and such.

He said afore they got finished they burnt Kelton's barn down.

I said was that a regular Fourth of July custom?

The shurff said hell no that was the only barn Kelton had.

I said I mean the fireworks.

The shurff said no Brayfuss donated the fireworks just that one year.

He said whole damn wagon-load.

He said it turned out to be quite some doings.

He said they cooked up a heifer and a horse.

I said they killed a horse for a barbecue?

The shurff said no he dropped dead pulling all them fireworks.

He said couldn't waste him.

He said you got to remember times was tough.

He said so was that goddam horse.

I shrugged.

I said it strikes me as being odd.

I said a man buys a wagon-load of fireworks and doesn't bother to watch any of them go off.

The shurff said oh Brayfuss done it fer the town-fokes.

He said he even give his clerk and his bartender the day off and he stayed behind and run the hotel all by hisself.

I said does Brayfuss own this hotel?

The shurff said Brayfuss owns everything in sight.

He took a long pull on the Sunnybrook.

He said well sir that was when all them rowdies popped in.

He said they got to carrying on something fierce what with threatening to burn the town down and rape the wimmen and what have you.

He said The Stranger was up in his room and they was raising such a ruckus he went down to see what was going on.

He said there was some harsh words and they got to

shooting and I reckon you already heard how it come out.

I said didn't anybody at the barbecue hear all the gunfire?

The shurff said they couldn't of heard it with them fireworks banging away.

He said Brayfuss buried the whole bunch afore anybody got back to town.

He said next morning Eddie Gee sang "On the Road to Mandalay" at the grave of The Stranger and that was that.

I said why "On the Road to Mandalay"?

The shurff said because that's the only song Eddie Gee knows.

He said he don't know but two verses of that.

I said who's Eddie Gee?

The shurff said he's the bartender at the hotel.

He said Eddie been bartender since alcohol got invented.

He said there is them what figger Eddie invented it.

I said is he a heavy drinker?

The shurff said Eddie only drinks one time a year but oh boy.

I said bad?

The shurff said bad ain't the word fer it.

He said hell there ain't no word fer it.

I said don't tell me he gets patriotic.

The shurff said no but it's damn near that bad.

He said last time Eddie got drunk he got holt of a pair of them water skis and he caught Jake Clausen going by in his pickup truck.

He said he got Jake to tow him up the street at fifty miles a hour.

I said how did it go?

The shurff said oh it went just fine till them skis caught fire.

I said do you still have the same desk clerk?

The shurff said no he moved to Philadelphia.

He said feller by the name of Darby.

The whiskey was almost half gone.

The shurff looked at the bottle and grinned ruefully.

He said don't reckon you want to keep just this little ole bit around.

I said no take it for your evidence file.

The shurff sat quietly for a time.

He said they made me shurff right after the trouble and ain't nothing happened since.

He said I keep hoping I'll make me just one real honest-to-God arrest afore I die.

He said something important.

He said like maybe a embezzler or a atheist or somebody.

I said well shurff crime waves come in cycles.

The shurff glanced up hopefully.

He said you sure of that?

I said yeah up in Chicago we get fifty cycles a day.

20

> ...seduction is merely a matter of somebody convincing you to convince them of what they been trying to convince you to convince them of all along...
>
> *Monroe D. Underwood*

I was half asleep when Brandy came in a few minutes short of midnight.

She sat on the bed and began to undress.

She said Purdue this is a rather strange area.

I said what was your first clue?

Brandy said you've noticed it too?

I said I noticed it before I left Chicago.

Brandy said I've just come from an outdoor religious service where they held a tongues-speaking contest.

I said what the hell were you doing at a religious service?

Brandy said chalk it up to curiosity for the moment.

She said the winner of the contest was disqualified but he really put on a show.

She said he came sprinting down the aisle and he threw himself onto the stage.

She said he jumped up and down and he rolled on the floor and in addition to speaking in a great many tongues he screamed oh Jesus Christ Almighty over and over again.

I shrugged.

I said yeah I guess they really get it on.

I said why did they disqualify him?

Brandy said he turned out to be the man from their Italian sausage concession.

She said he had a piece of live charcoal in his sock.

I said well I can see how that might fire him up just a bit.

Brandy slipped into bed.

Her lilac perfume drifted over me.

She kissed me.

She said hi there.

I said fancy meeting you here.

Brandy kissed me again.

She said I don't know about you but I'm becoming sexually aroused.

I said but you've only been in bed ten seconds.

I said I got a hunch you were born sexually aroused.

Brandy said no but I didn't waste much time getting at it.

She kissed me again.

She said just once around the pond Purdue.

I said look I got to go to a baseball practice in the morning.

Brandy kissed me again.

She said Purdue you're driving me crazy.

I said Brandy I haven't done anything yet.

Brandy said I knew damn well something was wrong.

She said do something.

I said like what?

Brandy said like just about anything.

I yawned.

Brandy threw her arms around me and began to squirm.

She said Purdue you satyr you've just seduced me again.

21

…it's a right-hander's world…which may be all that's wrong with it…

Monroe D. Underwood

At seven o'clock Rube's voice came from the hall.

He said how about breakfast?

I said okay I'll meet you in the lobby in fifteen minutes.

Brandy snuggled up tight.

She whispered the hell you will.

I met Rube and Moose in forty-five minutes.

We walked to the diner through a picture-book morning.

The sky was blue satin with cotton clouds hardly larger than ack-ack puffs.

Our backs were warm from the sun and our shoes were wet from the dew.

We were two hundred and twenty-five miles from Chicago but it could have been a million.

When we entered the diner the shurff was working on a

mug of coffee and chatting with Cemetery Carson.

He said I heard them Brady twins got all likkered up over in Jericho Ridge last night.

Cemetery said yeah they shot out all the streetlights and when the constable got there they was blazing away at the moon.

He said George Brady claimed he hit it three times.

He said ole George just couldn't figger out how come it stayed lit.

Rube nudged me.

He said do you begin to get the same faint impression I am beginning to get?

I shrugged.

I said that would depend on just what sort of faint impression you are beginning to get.

Rube said I am beginning to get the faint impression that things is done sort of differently in this part of the country.

Cemetery Carson said you fellers want eggs?

Rube said is they fresh?

Cemetery said well we do the best we can.

He stepped into a room next to the grill.

We heard a lot of wild screeching and cackling and flapping.

Cemetery emerged from a cloud of flying white feathers with a half-dozen eggs.

Rube nudged me.

He said you see what I mean?

He said back home people never keep chickens in the kitchen.

He said they keeps 'em in the bedroom where they belongs.

Moose said sure saves on alarm clocks.

I shrugged.

Rube caught Cemetery's eye.

He said say do you know anything about these Stranger City ballplayers?

Cemetery said oh sure most of 'em was over at Powersville where Duffy Slurff was managing last year.

Rube said how can I get in touch with this Duffy Slurff?

The shurff said they locked Duffy up last September.

Rube said what jail is he in?

Cemetery said well he ain't exactly in jail.

He said long about August ole Duffy started coming to the games wearing a black cloak and a big slouch hat.

The shurff said he got to swishing around and laughing sort of spooky like.

Cemetery said yeah he hauled out a brace of forty-five pistols and blowed the roof clean off the locker room.

He said he claimed his name was Lamont Cranston.

Rube scratched his jowl and stared into his coffee cup.

The shurff said some of the players was at East Cherry Creek until the manager had that run of tough luck.

Rube said long losing streak?

Cemetery said well what happened was he ate a whole bunch of sleeping pills probly thinking they was candy.

The shurff said I reckon they made him kind of groggy so I guess he got them cuts on his wrists whilst he was loading that ole shotgun which must of gone off by mistake.

Cemetery said they figger that was when he tripped and fell in that bathtub full of acid what had all them stray electric wires in.

The shurff said funny thing about them gas burners being turned on.

Cemetery said did anybody ever find out how all that gasoline caught fire in the basement?

The shurff said no and they never understood what that case of dynamite was doing in the parlor.

Moose said that feller better be more careful in the future.

Cemetery said would you believe it happened the very night they tole him he was going to manage at Stranger City this season?

We ate in silence.

After a while Rube said how many left-handers you reckon I got?

Cemetery said oh they is all left-handed.

Rube nudged me.

He said there just ain't nothing like good ole rural humor.

He turned back to Cemetery.

He said what you really mean is they is all left-handed except the catcher and three or four infielders and some pitchers.

The shurff said no that ain't what he really meant.

He said what he really meant was they is all lefthanded.

Rube nudged me.

He said only trouble with good ole rural humor is there is times when it is funny and there is times when it ain't.

He said this is one of the latter.

He lit a cigar and his Zippo trembled noticeably.

Cemetery said you got yourself one hell of a pitcher.

He said name of Timothy Glumphwick.

He said most fokes call him Tim on account of Tim is short for Timothy.

The shurff said he can really bring it.

Cemetery said *ooo-eee*.

The shurff said he struck out over three hunnert last year.

Rube said how many did he walk?

Cemetery said six hunnert and ninety-two.

The shurff said he hit a hunnert and thirty-eight with baseballs.

Cemetery said no it was only a hunnert and thirty-six because two was umpires.

The shurff said that's right.

He said kilt one and maimed one fer life.

Rube spilled a bit of his coffee.

He said foul tips?

Cemetery said no they was umpiring at first base.

Rube said pickoff plays?

The shurff said no there wasn't nobody on base neither time.

Rube's brown eyes were dilated.

His cigar was in ribbons.

His voice was fuzzy.

He said how many teams in this league?

Cemetery said two.

The shurff said us and Creepy Hollow.

Cemetery said they play all the games in Stranger City.

The shurff said that's because baseball is illegal in Creepy Hollow.

Rube stood up slowly.

He clutched the counter top.

He said well boys let's get out to the ball yard.

He said a feller could laugh hisself plumb to death over all this good ole rural humor.

22

…you show me a man what is allus watching birds
and I'll show you a man with a crick in his neck…

Monroe D. Underwood

Stranger City had the sweetest little ball park in the world.

It was old but carefully manicured and lovingly painted.

It cuddled close to the foot of a high green hill at the south end of town.

A low-roofed ten-row grandstand ran briefly down the baselines to drop abruptly into the five-row open-bench seating that continued to the walls and then into center field.

I calculated capacity to be in the vicinity of twenty-five hundred.

Rube and Moose and Count Frazzlewitz headed for the clubhouse and I started up the hill.

It was a tough climb.

Something like two hundred feet at a forty-five-degree pitch.

The nights in Wallace's tavern hadn't done my wind any

big favors.

At the top I found myself confronted by The Stranger.

He stood on an enormous granite block to tower some twenty feet above me.

He was thrice life-size and green with age and covered with bird droppings.

He was impressive as hell.

His craggy face was a mask of fury and his eyes were hate-filled slits.

His lips were peeled back from his teeth in a wolfish snarl.

His huge six-guns were held at hip-level in clawlike hands that could have throttled a tyrannosaur.

Affixed to his granite block was an engraved bronze plate.

HERE SLEEPS THE STRANGER FROM WHOSE GIANT SHADOW EMERGED STRANGER CITY A PROUD AND PEACEFUL PLACE TO LIVE.

I turned to look down over the little lilac town with its six or eight business buildings and its tidy tree-lined streets with red-shingled white bungalows.

I could make out the shurff's blue Model A and Brandy's silver-gray Porsche.

I ambled toward a densely wooded area that crowned the hilltop.

It shot up suddenly in poplar and pin oak and pine and from it poured a shrill torrent of sound.

Birds.

Feathered fury advising me to get out and stay out.

As I approached the forest the din grew more strident.

Then it stopped.

Under the trees I found a cathedral coolness.

The rocks were mossy and the sun managed only a few

ineffectual penetrations.

Then I stepped into blinding sunlight and the birds got back to cussing me out.

I had reached a narrow open span on a rocky ledge.

I walked to its lip and looked down.

I drew back instinctively.

Far far below was a sullen yellow river.

I was standing on the edge of Darby's Jump Off and I knew why Darby hadn't jumped.

…there is lots more ants than there is people… which is probly a very good thing for people…

Monroe D. Underwood

The pitchers loosened up in the right field corner and the outfielders shagged fly balls in left field and the lefthanded infield was hard at work.

Rube and I watched the activity through the backstop screen.

I said I wonder who ever assembled an all left-handed baseball team.

Rube scowled darkly.

He said well first off you almost got to assume he was left-handed.

I said what's more he had to be crazy.

Rube said all left-handers is crazy.

I said where does that put switch-hitters?

Rube said switch-hitters is usually confused transvestites.

I said I didn't know that.

Rube said neither did I till I figgered it out.

He said in Scranton I had a switch-hitting outfielder what had a two-foot beard and wore a purple brassiere with rhinestones.

I said could he hit?

Rube said I'll never know.

He said the sonofabitch eloped with my shortstop.

I said Rube you have a catcher out there with a bad limp.

Rube nodded.

He said yeah I better talk to that kid.

The catcher's name was Gaylord Messerschmitt.

He was a slender boy with piercing gray-green eyes.

Rube said son it looks like you got a charley horse.

Gaylord Messerschmitt said no I got a wooden leg.

Rube smiled patiently.

He said now young feller I only got me a couple days to get this outfit ready for a opener so leave us save such wild hilarity for the shower room.

Gaylord Messerschmitt said I never take showers.

He said showers would warp my wooden leg.

Rube gave Gaylord Messerschmitt a very frosty stare.

He said that's twice.

Gaylord Messerschmitt sighed resignedly.

He removed his shin guards.

He spiked himself savagely in the left leg.

Splinters flew in all directions.

Rube stepped back and brushed wood fragments from the front of his shirt.

He said well son I don't mean to discourage you none but I just got to tell you flat out that left-handed catchers with wooden legs ain't in particularly great demand this season.

He said furthermore I got some pretty strong reservations

about next season.

Moose had arrived.

He said hey a catcher with two wooden legs wouldn't need no shin guards.

Rube nudged me.

He said Moose don't say much but you got to admit he makes some mighty pertinent observations.

Gaylord Messerschmitt said what if I was the only catcher in the world?

He said what if all the other catchers went to a convention and it got wiped out by a bomb?

He said you just better consider that.

Rube said I will son I will.

Rube shook his head.

He said it would take a left-handed catcher to think like that.

He squinted into the left field corner.

He said there's a pitcher down there what is wilder than a tiger with a knot in its tail.

Moose said who would tie a knot in a tiger's tail?

Rube said at the moment his name eludes me.

Moose said well if he keeps it up he gonna get reported to the SPCA.

He said where will that catchers' convention be held?

The pitcher stood about six-eleven.

He may have weighed one-fifty and he had bushy hayloft hair and a great many teeth that protruded in approximately the same number of directions.

We stood behind him as he leaned back and fogged a pitch that ripped out a row of benches in the right field seats.

Rube tapped him on the shoulder.

He said boy what's your name?

The pitcher said Timothy Glumphwick.

He said some fokes calls me Tim since Tim is short for Timothy you see.

Rube said well Tim maybe you better ease up just a mite because we don't want to got to send to Canada to get your arm back.

Timothy Glumphwick said oh I'm only throwing soft stuff today.

Rube said well what was that last pitch?

Timothy Glumphwick said that was my change-up.

He said you wanna see my hummer?

Rube wheeled and headed for left field.

He was pale.

We crossed the green expanse of outfield and watched the fungo hitter loft the ball high into the blue June sky.

Horsefish Hallahan and Sorehead Hawkins and Barnaby Klutz converged at high speeds.

Rube covered his eyes.

Moose dropped to one knee and made the sign of the cross.

There was a sickening thud.

Like gasoline fumes igniting.

About three thousand gallons' worth.

The ball plummeted to earth and bounced to the wall.

Rube walked to the scene of impact and studied his three prostrate outfielders.

He said who said baseball ain't no contact sport?

We went in to watch infield practice.

Rube's eyes were glued on the kid at third base.

He said I like that youngster's looks even if he is left-handed.

Rube had spotted a good one.

The boy made diving stops left and right.

He went high for liners and came down like a ballet dancer.

He sucked up ground balls like a vacuum cleaner.

He had a rifle arm and his throws were right on the money.

Rube waved and the third baseman came on the run.

He was Japanese.

He bowed and said good morning Mr. Mountainstir.

Rube said you're the first ballplayer I've seen in four years.

The third baseman said my name Isoroku Yabuki.

He said my father teach me arr I know.

He said my father very fine barr prayer.

He said you hear of great dubber pray combination Yabuki to Watsuki to Fishstein?

Moose said who was that last guy?

Rube said skip it Moose.

We reached the second-base area just in time to see shortstop Dudley Shift range far to his right to flag down a sizzling ground ball.

He fired to second baseman Opus Ganderneck who took the throw as he crossed the second-base bag.

Opus Ganderneck flipped the ball back to Dudley Shift who blazed it to first baseman Attila Honeywell.

Rube skidded to a stop with his arms raised defensively like a fighter teetering on the brink of a TKO.

He grabbed Moose's elbow.

He said Moose please tell me that I haven't just witnessed what I'm absolutely certain I've just witnessed.

Moose said well if you've just witnessed a short to second to short to first double play then you are witnessing just dandy.

Rube called Opus Ganderneck over to him.

He put his hand on the second baseman's shoulder.

He spoke in calm and fatherly fashion.

He said now son I only got me about fifty years in this game so I am probly unfamiliar with its more sophisticated points therefore I would be interested in learning why you didn't throw that little round white thing to first base like you should of instead of back to the shortstop like you shouldn't of.

Opus Ganderneck said because I am left-handed.

He said the last time I made the double play pivot I busted my collarbone and got a triple hernia.

Dudley Shift said last year we almost pulled that play in a exhibition game here.

Opus Ganderneck said yeah it would of worked if Attila Honeywell had been in position to take the throw.

Rube frowned.

He said where was Attila Honeywell?

Dudley Shift said well at that particular moment Attila Honeywell was engaged in an all-out brawl with about thirty million big black ants.

Attila Honeywell had moved into the conference.

He was a haggard young man with deep dark circles under his eyes.

He said I beg your pardon.

He said in the interests of accuracy it must be noted here that it wasn't thirty million big black ants.

He said this is because it was ninety-six million big black ants.

Moose said hell what's sixty-six million big black ants one way or the other?

Attila Honeywell's haunted eyes bulged.

He said well baby you just get sixty-six million big black ants in your jockstrap and you are absolutely certain to find out.

Rube said where do these big black ants come from?

Attila Honeywell said they got a commune or some

goddam thing over by first base.

He said they are holding a election.

Rube chewed on his cigar for a moment.

He inched cautiously toward Attila Honeywell.

He said tell me son how do you know they is holding a election?

Attila Honeywell said because they are galloping around carrying a bunch of teeny-weeny signs.

Moose said well that don't got to mean it's a election.

He said maybe it's a football rally.

Opus Ganderneck said it don't figger to be no football rally.

He said hell this is baseball season.

Rube said what do these teeny-weeny signs say?

Attila Honeywell said the print is too small for me to read.

Dudley Shift said do you ever hear any speeches?

Attila Honeywell said I wouldn't know if I did.

He said I probly wouldn't understand a word the little bastards say.

Opus Ganderneck said I wonder what language ants speak.

Dudley Shift said ant I bet.

Moose said yeah but there is so many kinds of ants.

Opus Ganderneck said man just think of all them dialects.

The center field flagpole came down with a thunderous splintering crash.

We turned to see Count Frazzlewitz standing triumphant at its severed base.

He smiled a German shepherd smile.

Rube stared at me.

He said the idle mind is the Devil's playground.

24

…a small town is where the man what don't drink is a sissy and the man what does is a drunkard…

Monroe D. Underwood

We walked toward the hotel without speaking.

A blazing sun rode high above Stranger City.

The little community was wilted and muted.

A yellow mongrel dog dozed in the shade of a huge silver maple.

He opened a glazed eye and flogged the ground with a ratty tail.

Dust flew.

A few sparrows frolicked in the street.

An old man soaked up sun on the park bench across from the hotel.

The old man who had sat there the day before.

He raised a hand to me.

He said Mr. Purdue I'd like to speak with you.

Rube nudged me.

He said that's Horatio Brayfuss.

He said Brayfuss owns most of this cookie jar.

He said maybe you better give him a couple minutes.

I went over to the park bench.

Brayfuss gave me a weary smile and a limp cold handshake.

He said pray be seated Mr. Purdue.

I sat.

Brayfuss said how do you like my city?

I said it's very nice sir.

Brayfuss gave me a skeptical look.

I said I was raised in a small town sir.

Brayfuss nodded and studied me.

At close range he was older than I had thought.

His white hair was thin and his cheeks were sunken.

His lips were withered.

Only his eyes seemed alive.

They were faded but lightning-quick and bead-bright.

If the eyes are windows of the soul Horatio Brayfuss was not a man to be taken lightly.

He was troubled by a hoarse racking cough that made my neck-hair curl.

It came frequently and it left him weak and gasping.

Brayfuss said Mr. Purdue I understand that you have expressed an interest in the legend of The Stranger.

I shrugged.

I said I guess I've heard most of it sir.

Brayfuss said are there any points that require clarification?

I said well not really sir.

I said except that he must have been mighty fast on the draw.

Brayfuss said his speed was beyond comprehension Mr. Purdue.

I said twelve men with twelve rounds?

Brayfuss said yes Mr. Purdue and each was shot through the buttonhole of his shirt pocket.

I said you buried them all sir?

Brayfuss said every damned one Mr. Purdue.

I said it must have been a hell of a job for one man sir.

Brayfuss said that it was Mr. Purdue that it was.

He turned slowly on the park bench.

His sharp old eyes twinkled and a corner of his withered mouth twitched.

He said Mr. Purdue do you doubt the story?

I shrugged.

I said sir why should I?

I said apparently nobody else has.

Brayfuss said Mr. Purdue you must understand one thing.

He said in those days this town was failing.

He said no one knew we were here.

He said The Stranger changed all that.

He said my hotel began to thrive.

He said my newspaper tripled its subscriptions.

He said my bank increased its operating capital tenfold.

He said my book sold over a hundred thousand copies.

I said what was the name of your book sir?

Brayfuss said the name of my book was *The Whole Stranger City Story.*

I said what sort of book was it sir?

Brayfuss said it was a coloring book.

I said I see.

Brayfuss said why do you ask?

I shrugged.

I said I just wondered.

Brayfuss leaned back and looked around him.

He said yes Mr. Purdue The Stranger brought new life to a dying community.

He said look at us now.

He said a diligent hustling bustling beehive of activity.

I shrugged.

Brayfuss said Mr. Purdue there are times when one man can alter the flow of history.

He said remember that if you will.

I said I'll do that sir.

Brayfuss winked at me.

He got up and hobbled southward.

His buckthorn cane struck little puffs of dust from the footpath.

25

> …oncet there was a song what nobody never heard before…come to think of it nobody never heard it since…
>
> *Monroe D. Underwood*

I caught up with Rube and Moose in the hotel lounge.

Rube was drinking a double bourbon and water and Moose was inhaling a few bottles of Old Washensachs.

Count Frazzlewitz was working on a table leg.

I sat next to Rube and ordered a hooker of Sunnybrook.

I said well Rube what do you think?

Rube said son if I was to tell you what I think your blood would run cold.

I said I'm talking about the baseball team.

Rube said so am I.

I said do you anticipate problems?

Rube said well I got to admit that the possibility has been stomping around in my mind.

Eddie Gee piled into the conversation.

He said I just can't wait until tomorry night.

Rube said what happens tomorry night?

Eddie said why the Fifteenth Annual Stranger City Baseball Ball that's what.

Rube said oh goody goody.

Eddie said it's the foremost social event of the year.

He said sometimes it goes on till damn near ten-thirty.

Rube said you people better slow down.

He said look what happened to Pompeii.

Moose said yeah the Japs bombed hell out of it.

We heard the shurff's car go by.

The barrel organ was pumping out its wistful melody.

Moose said what's the name of that song?

Eddie said I don't got the slightest idea.

Moose said I never heard of that one.

He said was it ever on the Hit Parade?

Eddie said was what ever on the Hit Parade?

Moose said " I Don't Got the Slightest Idea."

Eddie said the title ain't familiar.

He said whistle me a couple bars.

Moose whistled a bit of the barrel organ tune.

He said that's it.

Eddie said that's what?

Moose said "I Don't Got the Slightest Idea."

Eddie said me neither.

Rube nudged me.

He said the Bible says you gotta reap what you sow.

He said but my God this is ridiculous.

When we passed through the lobby the desk clerk waved us down.

He said have you gents heard the good news?

Rube said no but I will be delighted to hear some.

He said in fact I will be so delighted there is an excellent chance I will have to be clapped in irons.

The desk clerk said the Bobby Crackers Blitzkrieg for Christ just hit Powersville and it will be in Stranger City Monday night.

Rube said well maybe that is good news.

He said but I'll lay five two and even it ain't.

26

…they ought to build a monument to Nixon…he was the only president what got caught doing what all the other presidents didn't get caught doing…

Monroe D. Underwood

Brandy had left a note on the bed.

PURDUE XXXX XXXXX OOOOO OOOO GONE TO POWERSVILLE XXXXX XXXX OOOOO OOOO SEE YOU TONIGHT XXXX XXXXX OOOOO OOOO RAISE MAIN MAST AND CLEAR DECKS FOR ACTION XXXX XXXXX OOO OOO XXXXX XXXX OOOOO OOOO BRANDY.

PS XXXXXXXXX OOOOOOOOO XXXXXXXXX OOOOOO

I shrugged.

I sprawled on the bed with a busted Camel.

I thought of Horatio Brayfuss and his diligent hustling bustling beehive of activity.

Dogs slept undisturbed along the main thoroughfare.

Sparrows played leapfrog in the middle of the street.

I had seen three motor vehicles since my arrival.

Brandy's Porsche and a fender-flapping pickup truck and the shurff's Model A.

I thought of the gruesome monument on the hilltop.

According to its bronze plate Stranger City was a peaceful place to live.

Well I'd go with that in essence but it really wasn't all that tranquil.

The village barkeep went waterskiing on dry land and the local law enforcement officer drove around with a barrel organ bleating in his wake.

I crushed my cigarette and fell asleep.

27

> ...oncet I knowed a man what went out to eat a grizzly bear and starved to death in a treetop...
>
> *Monroe D. Underwood*

I slept like a drugged man.

I came out of it at sundown.

I was splashing cold water on my face when Rube knocked on the door.

He said I'm so hungry I could eat a grizzly bear.

I said me too.

Rube said I mean raw.

I said okay where can we get a couple raw grizzly bears?

Rube said I don't know but Moose got a line on a Chinese joint over on a side street.

He said a place called Sun Mat Soo's.

I said any old port in a storm.

During the walk to Sun Mat Soo's Rube said Moose is nuts about Chinese restaurants.

He said he likes to agitate the waitresses.

He said he always orders sweet-sour dragon tonsils.

I shrugged.

I said they're better deep-fried.

Rube said yeah more tender.

Sun Mat Soo's was a small meticulously clean place.

When we entered there wasn't a soul in sight.

We took a corner table.

Rube sat with his back to the kitchen commanding a full view of the front door.

He said I always like to watch the people come in.

Moose said nice thing about sitting that way is you also get to see 'em go out.

Moose looked at the bead curtains.

He said hey Rube looky all the bead curtains.

Rube said Confucius say hungry man always look at menu not bead curtains.

Moose said well screw Confucius.

He said Confucius probly gets to see bead curtains all the time.

A woman came out of the kitchen.

She was sixty or so.

She was about five feet tall and she couldn't have weighed an ounce over ninety-five pounds.

She had crisp curly gray hair and violet eyes.

In her day she had been a real looker.

She still was.

Her violet eyes were bright with merriment.

She signaled for silence with a finger to her lips.

She tiptoed up behind Rube and clapped her hands over his eyes.

She said guess who Rube.

Rube's jaw went slack.

He said Frankenstein's great-grandmother.

He said I hope.

The violet-eyed lady said guess again.

Rube slumped in his chair.

He said it just ain't no use.

He said Tillie Zilch.

Tillie laughed happily.

She said I knew you'd be in sooner or later.

She said I got the last waitress job in town.

She said good thing I speak Chinese.

Rube said Tillie I bet you could get a whole lot of jobs in China.

Moose was grinning.

He said plittee lady you gottee sweetee-souree dlagon tonsils?

Rube said Moose this is Tillie Zilch.

He said you pulled that dragon tonsil routine on her before.

Moose said oh yeah Tillie Zilch.

He smiled forlornly.

He said I wonder is there any other Chinese restaurants in town.

Tillie threw a smooth lightly tanned arm around Rube's neck.

It displayed a large tattoo that read Tillie Loves Rube.

Tillie said Rube I've been with you every year since you managed Beaver Dam and I worked the Jade Garden in North Livershank.

Rube nodded numbly.

He said thirty-goddam-nine seasons.

Tillie said you didn't think I'd miss this one did you?

Rube said well a feller got a right to hope.

He said you could look it up in the Constitution.

He said I got a copy in my room.

He said I'll go get it.

Tillie Zilch sat on Rube's knee.

She looked for all the world like a perky violet-eyed doll.

She said Rube why didn't you stay at Fletcher's Crossing?

Rube said I got fired.

Tillie winked at me.

She said he didn't get fired.

She said he quit to get away from me.

She kissed Rube on the ear.

She said it didn't work.

She said he tries it every year and it never works.

She kissed Rube on the forehead.

She said isn't that right Rube?

Rube groaned.

Tillie said you boys want chow mein as usual?

Rube said I seem to of lost my appetite.

Tillie flitted into the kitchen.

Rube nudged me.

He said honest to God I thought I had brung it off this time.

He said who the hell ever heard of Stranger City?

He said it ain't on the map.

He said an Injun tracker would get lost trying to find it.

He said when God destroys the world He's gonna miss it altogether.

I shrugged.

I said Tillie seems like a fine lady.

Rube said there just ain't no finer lady than Tillie.

I said then what's wrong with her?

Rube said there's only two things wrong with Tillie.

He said the first thing is Tillie is bound and determined to get married.

He said the second thing is she's bound and determined to get married to me.

I shrugged.

I said well is that the worst thing that could happen to you?

Rube said maybe not but it comes close enough to get in the finals.

Tillie returned with our chow mein.

We heard the shurff go by with his barrel organ.

Moose said Tillie what's the name of that song?

Tillie said it beats me.

Moose said I never heard of no song by that name.

Rube dropped his fork and held up a warning hand.

He said let's call the whole thing off.

Tillie said oh gracious Rube that's not it.

She said Fred Astaire sang "Let's Call the Whole Thing Off" in a 1937 movie.

She said we saw it at the Custard Corners Rialto and you had your cheek on my shoulder.

Rube said sure I had my cheek on your shoulder.

He said I had a toothache and we just got done blowing a double-header to Vinegar Valley.

He said you can't expect a man to act rational under such circumstances.

Tillie rumpled Rube's hair.

She said Rube you should surrender.

Rube said that's what they kept telling Winston Churchill.

Tillie giggled.
She said Rube that's a lousy parallel.
Rube said I know it.
He said all Churchill had to worry about was Hitler.

28

...I get the feeling I have lived this moment before every damn time the bartender says no credit...

Monroe D. Underwood

We left Sun Mat Soo's after dark.

Clouds obscured the moon and trees rustled in a damp gentle wind.

There was muted thunder to the southwest.

When we reached the hotel Rube said I'll buy a drink providing there ain't no crazy talk.

Eddie Gee smiled hello from behind the bar.

Rube ordered a triple bourbon with water and Moose took a bottle of Old Washensachs.

I had a jolt of Sunnybrook.

Eddie said maybe you guys can help.

He said I just bought a second-hand Ford and on one of the hubcaps it says GM.

He said that don't make no sense.

He said what does GM stand for?

Moose said which hubcap?

Eddie said why?

Moose said it might be real important.

Eddie said oh.

He said right rear.

Moose said it stands for general manager.

Eddie said I think you mean General MacArthur.

Moose said General MacArthur got fired.

Eddie said yes and this came as a severe shock to a great many people.

He said one of which was General MacArthur.

Moose said General MacArthur uttered the immortal words old soldiers never die they just fade away.

Eddie said he also uttered the immortal words I shall return.

Moose said who was it uttered the immortal words damn the torpedoes full speed ahead?

Eddie said well whoever he was he sure didn't know much about torpedoes.

Rube nudged me.

He said did you ever get that funny feeling you have lived this moment afore?

I said why sure.

Rube said well I just got that funny feeling.

I said okay so tell me what happens next.

Rube said son I didn't have the guts to stick around and find out what happened the first time.

I followed Rube up the stairs.

When he closed his door I could hear him jamming a chair under the knob.

> …oncet I had a typewriter what made all kinds of mistakes…
>
> *Monroe D. Underwood*

The cloudburst struck just after eleven o'clock.

It came with the savage suddenness of a Solomon Islands storm.

Thunder raved and chanted through the skies.

Wild jagged sheets of brilliant blue lightning ripped the cauliflower clouds to confetti.

Stranger City was buried under the onslaught.

Brandy came in at the peak of the thing.

She dripped like a busted spigot.

She cussed quietly but with maximum efficiency.

I said did you get your half-slip wet?

Brandy said Purdue I don't mind a bit of water.

She said it's all in the game.

She said what tees me off is I was closing in on something

when this goddam rain interfered.

Brandy went into the bathroom and turned on the light.

She left the door open and she peeled and draped her soaked clothing over the shower curtain rod.

I sat in bed and watched.

It was one hell of a show.

Brandy said I was at a religious service this afternoon.

She said the preacher held a faith-healing session for twenty-five middle-aged men who suffered from sexual impotency.

I said were they healed?

Brandy said I really don't know but right after the session two dozen women and one man were raped.

She said it was the very first time the preacher had been raped.

She said he didn't particularly care for it.

I shrugged.

I said well some like it and some don't.

I said so what did you do tonight?

Brandy said I went to another religious service.

She said it grew increasingly interesting until the rain.

I said Brandy what's with this sudden religious kick?

Brandy said only time will tell.

She said how did the baseball practice go?

I said possibly worse than the faith-healing session.

Brandy said no.

I said yes.

Brandy said have you worked on your report to Chericola?

I said I just remembered I don't have a typewriter.

I said I also remembered I don't know how to type.

Brandy said I have a portable in the car.

She said you dictate and I'll type it for you.

She was standing naked in the bathroom doorway.

Her hands were on her hips.
Her chorus-girl legs were spread ever so slightly.
Sort of a seafaring pose.
I said I like that stance.
I said you could pass for a pirate.
Brandy said I'm a love pirate.
She turned out the bathroom light.
She said prepare to be boarded.
She wasn't kidding.

30

> . . . a gigolo is a man what gets paid for doing what any idiot would be perfeckly willing to do for nothing. . .
>
> *Monroe D. Underwood*

On Sunday morning Stranger City was a sodden mess.

Broken tree limbs cluttered the area and the park across the street was partially underwater.

Stranger Avenue was choked with mist and the rain was still falling.

I took one look and went back to bed.

Brandy said will there be a baseball practice?

I said not unless they hold one in the lobby.

Brandy sat up and lit a pair of cigarettes.

She gave one to me.

She said Purdue I hate to see this come to an end.

I said I wasn't aware that it was coming to an end.

Brandy said yes I suppose it will be all wrapped up by the middle of the week.

She said it's been much too simple dammit.

She said Purdue when we get back to Chicago I want you to work with me.

I said as what?

I said detective or gigolo?

Brandy put out our cigarettes.

She pushed me onto my back.

She popped up onto me with her knees straddling my chest.

She said does it really make a difference?

She looked down at me and laughed silently.

She said the pay rate's the same.

...coffee is something what looks like tar and tastes even worse and nobody can possibly do without...

Monroe D. Underwood

At ten there was a light knock on the door.

It was Rube.

He handed me two steaming containers of coffee.

I said two?

Rube grinned.

He said hell you never know.

He said you just might get company.

…chess is a game in which the only way you can jump the queen is it you're a knight…

Monroe D. Underwood

At noon we heard a pounding on Rube's door.

We heard Tillie say Rube Mountainstill either you are coming out here or I am coming in there.

Rube said well if that is the answer I would sure hate to hear the question.

Tillie said Rube you open the door this very minute.

Rube said Tillie it just ain't safe.

Tillie said what are you doing in there?

Rube said I am playing chess with some great big hairy African lion.

Tillie said oh why don't you just give up and get it over with?

Rube said why should I give up?

He said I'm gonna checkmate him in a couple more moves.

Tillie said Rube you need me.

She said we need each other.
Rube said your move Leo.

...oncet I knowed a man what got nefarious but a few penicillin shots cleared it up before his wife found out...

Monroe D. Underwood

The weather cleared by late afternoon.

Brandy said well Purdue I don't like to break this magic spell but both of us are weak from hunger.

I said in my case it's more than hunger.

Brandy said you have a baseball ball to attend and I must make one more trip to Powersville.

She said I'll see you tonight and I'll come to the ball game tomorrow.

I said what's so hot in Powersville?

Brandy said there are nefarious forces hard at work there.

I said holy Christ.

Brandy said oddly enough you have hit the nail right on the head.

She said the Destroy America Destroy America bastards are back and they're flying a brand-new banner.

I said are you talking about DADA?

Brandy said I certainly am.

She said what would you like to know?

I said I'd like to know what nefarious means.

34

> …a war of attrition begins when your mother-in-law discovers where you hid your bottle…
>
> *Monroe D. Underwood*

When Brandy was gone I tapped on Rube's door.

I said could you handle another order of chow mein?

Rube said I could handle the chow mein but there ain't no way I could handle Tillie Zilch.

I said okay I'll meet you in the lounge before the baseball ball.

Rube said I been trying to figger me a way of getting out of that thing.

He said I got a premonition this is going to be a night what will live in infamy.

I said Rube you're the manager and you're stuck.

Rube said boy you just ain't much help at all.

Stranger City sparkled in six o'clock sunshine and the walk was pleasant.

The shurff went by with his barrel organ fluttering its

happy-sad song.

He waved.

At Sun Mat Soo's Tillie was seated at a table.

She was paging through a wedding gown catalog.

I sat opposite her.

I said who's getting married?

Tillie said Rube is.

I said does Rube know about this?

Tillie said of course he knows.

She said he just hates to face up to it.

She said do you know what a war of attrition is?

I said no.

The corners of Tillie's violet eyes crinkled with her smile.

She said that's where I have the advantage.

She said neither does Rube.

She said he'll throw in the towel any minute now.

I said Tillie how long have you waged this war of attrition?

Tillie's smile faded.

She said thirty-nine years.

I said how's the chow mein today?

Tillie said you'll be the first to know.

When she brought my dinner she said do you know how many baseballs Rube Mountainstill has autographed for me?

She said five thousand two hundred and thirty-one that's how many.

She said I get an autographed ball every time I go to a game.

I said apparently you don't miss many games.

Tillie said two so far.

She said one was when my mother died.

I said what about the other one?

Tillie said when my father died.

She said I got every damn ball back home.

She said I got baseballs on the mantel and baseballs in the chandeliers and baseballs in the basement.

She said I got baseballs in the refrigerator and baseballs under the bed.

She said you never saw so many baseballs in your life.

She said all they ever say is To Tillie From Rube.

She said I'd trade the entire collection for just one that said To Tillie With Love From Rube.

Tillie picked up her wedding gown catalog and headed for the kitchen.

Her shoulders were bent and shaking.

My heart went out to her.

35

> …Mandalay is a place where the dawn comes up like thunder after you been out playing like them flying fishes…same as Chicago in that respect…
>
> *Monroe D. Underwood*

The Fifteenth Annual Stranger City Baseball Ball was to be held in the Stranger City firehouse.

We strolled in that direction with Count Frazzlewitz bringing up the rear.

It was a balmy evening and Stranger City's great butteryellow moon was clearing the distant trees.

Rube stopped to watch the stars being turned on.

He said I live in a town even smaller than this.

Moose said how many fokes Rube?

Rube said how many ain't important.

He said it's what kind.

He said these is good fokes.

Moose said don't nobody never take no census?

Rube said well one of them census fellers come to town back in sixty.

He said damn fool cut acrost Cy Danby's west pasture.

Rube put a match to a fresh cigar and blew smoke at the stars.

It was the beginning of a lengthy silence.

At last Moose said hey Rube was that the end of the story?

Rube said goddam near.

He said Cy Danby had the meanest bull in Greenbrier County.

We crossed the road and entered the firehouse.

The interior of the old building was bright with hundreds of colored streamers and banners that said PLAY BALL

Horatio Brayfuss limped directly to us.

On his lapel was a silver ribbon imprinted with HELLO NEIGHBOR.

He said gentlemen Stranger City bids you welcome.

Moose smiled expansively.

He said well the feeling is mutual I will bet you fifty-seven dollars.

Rube said cool it Moose.

Brayfuss said you will find refreshments at the bar and dance music will begin shortly.

We drifted in the direction of a makeshift bar located in front of a weary old fire engine.

A huge placard rested against the windshield of the exhausted machine.

It read GO STRANGERS GO.

Moose looked at it.

He said this town got a very inhospitable attitude if you ask me.

Rube said well Moose nobody asked you in the first place and Strangers is the name of our ball club in the second place.

Moose said how did we get in second place when the season ain't even got started yet?

Rube nudged me.

He said I spend most of my time somewheres betwixt suicide and murder.

He said right about here it looks like murder.

Moose said aw Rube I wouldn't murder nobody over no beat-up ole placard.

He said you got to remember these is just simple country fokes.

Horatio Brayfuss was coming our way with his buckthorn cane clacking on the concrete floor.

He said the mayor of Stranger City is most anxious to meet you.

He steered us toward an elderly couple who awaited us with plastic smiles.

Brayfuss introduced them as Mayor Gordon Fitzhugh and his utterly charming wife Gilda Fitzhugh.

Moose muttered something about both of them having exactly the same last names.

Rube muttered something about Moose not criticizing local customs.

Gordon Fitzhugh was the most average man I had ever met.

There was absolutely nothing noticeable about him.

He was a man you couldn't have identified if he had held you up at high noon on the courthouse steps with a 90mm antiaircraft gun.

Gilda Fitzhugh was another matter.

I put her at approximately three hundred pounds.

Her strawberry blonde hairdo was two feet tall.

When you added this to Gilda and her four-inch spike heels you ended up with a formidable-looking female more than eight feet in height.

In her silver-sequined bright red dress she bore a marked resemblance to the old fire truck.

Moose noticed this.

He muttered something about which is which.

Rube muttered something unprintable.

Brayfuss muttered something about Gilda Fitzhugh being very big in the writing field.

Moose muttered something about Gilda Fitzhugh being very big in just about any old field.

He muttered something about Soldier Field.

Rube muttered something about wishing to Christ Moose would shut up.

Gilda Fitzhugh said Mr. Mountainstill I am the Stranger City correspondent for the Chicago *Globe* and I will be doing an in-depth article on the opening of our baseball season.

She said oh I'm just so thrilled and I'll hardly know the first thing to do when I sit in the Stranger City dugout tomorrow.

Rube said well ma'am when you sit in the Stranger City dugout tomorrow the first thing to do will be get out of the Stranger City dugout on account of reporters ain't allowed in the Stranger City dugout.

Gilda Fitzhugh's reply was sidetracked by Eddie Gee who went by doing handstands and singing "On the Road to Mandalay."

Moose said hey Rube there is one hell of a act.

Rube said oh I wouldn't say that.

He said he just blowed that second line all to hell.

He said it's flying fishes not frying shishes.

Moose said I never heard of no Mandalay.

He said what the hell league they in?

Rube said it wouldn't work Moose.

He said Tillie would find us.

Brayfuss moved us around.

We were introduced to Doctor Burnham and Ike Kelton and any number of Stranger City's prominent citizens.

Brayfuss said Mr. Mountainstill when you mentioned a Count Frazzlewitz I thought you were bringing a friend.

Rube said you was right.

He said I ain't never had no friend like The Count.

He said by the way where is The Count?

Rube whistled and in an instant Tillie Zilch had him in a bear hug.

She said all right you flirtatious rascal what can I do for you?

Rube said well you can start out by getting me booked on the first rocket to Saturn.

Count Frazzlewitz appeared.

He was dragging the stub of a freshly mangled fire ladder.

Eddie Gee went by again.

This time he was balancing his false teeth on his nose.

Gilda Fitzhugh said oh how I detest that horrid man.

Eddie's balancing act carried him in several directions.

His false teeth teetered precariously.

Eddie picked up speed and stayed under them until they plopped into the punch bowl.

Gilda Fitzhugh threw up her hands and screamed oh dear God this is terrible.

Rube said well it might of been worse only I can't think of how.

A six-piece combo struck up a dance tune.

Rube said this is the first combo I ever seen with three bass fiddles.

The bass fiddles took a chorus.

Rube said they sound like a bull crocodile what got trapped in a revolving door.

Moose said well I got to admit I never heard of no bull crocodile getting trapped in a revolving door.

Rube said Moose that was just a comparison I thunk of.

Moose said I just can't figger how a bull crocodile could get trapped in a revolving door.

Rube said don't mess with it Moose it is bad for your mind.

Eddie Gee came weaving up to us.

He said wash ish big problum here?

Moose said did you ever hear a bull crocodile what got trapped in a revolving door?

Eddie Gee said oh yesh thousansh timesh.

He said they shound eggshackle like thish.

He let out an earsplitting bellow.

Gilda Fitzhugh departed the planet.

On her way down she shrieked if somebody will murder this menace I will gladly go to jail for it.

Rube nudged me.

He said I can't hardly wait to get back to my little house in Greenbrier County and look out the window and watch it snow.

Moose said is that all there is to do in Greenbrier County?

Rube said no Moose sometimes it rains.

The six-piece combo played "Take Me Out to the Ball Game."

The bandleader stepped to the microphone.

He said friends and neighbors it is time that I introduce the man who will manage the Stranger City Strangers to the pennant.

Eddie Gee staggered and spilled his schooner of beer down the back of Gilda Fitzhugh's bright red dress.

Gilda Fitzhugh let out a Comanche war whoop.

The crowd followed her lead and cheered wildly.

Rube acknowledged the tribute by hastily gulping his bourbon on the rocks.

The band played "Moonlight and Roses."

Tillie Zilch threw herself into Rube's arms.

She said oh Rube they're playing our song.

Rube said that couldn't be our song.

He said there ain't no minors in it.

Gilda Fitzhugh gave a bloodcurdling scream.

Eddie Gee was coming down the firepole.

He was stark naked except for a Stranger City fireman's helmet.

He was waving a gleaming fire ax.

He hopped into the old fire engine and started the motor.

He turned on the siren and the bell.

He ran over the makeshift bar.

He almost ran over Gilda Fitzhugh.

He drove into a wall.

There was a muffled explosion.

Flames broke out.

Gilda Fitzhugh hollered for God's sake call the fire department.

Rube nudged me.

He said we better leave.

He said there's liable to be trouble here.

36

…oncet I knowed a man what got kilt playing hopscotch…he swallowed his mouthpiece…

Monroe D. Underwood

It was one o'clock in the morning.

I said Brandy what in the hell are we accomplishing down here?

I said Chericola got a ball club that couldn't whip the Little Sisters of the Poor.

I said if the entire town turned out for every game it couldn't support a hopscotch team.

I said you're on some kind of religious bender and I'm stumbling around like a goddam zombie wondering what's going on.

Brandy said Purdue please let's not talk just now.

She said let's finish what we're doing.

I said hell I'm not even sure I'm doing that right.

Brandy said you're doing it right Purdue.

She said take my word for it you're doing it right.

She said oh my God are you ever doing it right.

I shrugged.

Brandy said dammit Purdue stop shrugging and keep on doing it right.

37

…well maybe tit ain't proper but I never heard of nobody ever getting their teat in the wringer…

Monroe D. Underwood

Ebbing twilight lapped gently at the windowsills.

Brandy said Purdue give me another twenty-four hours.

I said don't be ridiculous.

I said another twenty-four minutes would kill me.

Brandy said I'm not talking about sex you nut.

She gave me an exasperated kiss.

She said that was an exasperated kiss.

I said I know it.

I said I know an exasperated kiss when I get one.

Brandy said I'm talking about throwing DADA for a big loss.

I said well you don't need me for that.

I said I'm about as useful as tits on a bull.

Brandy said teats.

I shrugged.

I said well whatever.

Brandy said Purdue you're very important.

She said you've given me the time I've needed to nail the DADA business down.

I said how did DADA get mixed up in this anyway?

Brandy said just sit tight and I'll explain following the Bobby Crackers Blitzkrieg for Christ.

She said you'll be going won't you?

I shrugged.

Brandy said oh Purdue don't miss it.

She said you'll never forget it.

38

…getting married is as easy as rolling off a log but it don't make nowhere near as much sense…

Monroe D. Underwood

On Monday morning I found Rube sitting alone on the park bench.

He said I just been doing some tall thinking and I got this here town all figgered out.

I sat beside him and lit a fishhook Camel.

I said let's hear your theory.

Rube said okay leave us consider the factors involved.

He said this is a town what don't got a church in sight.

I said I'd noticed that.

Rube said this town holds baseball balls on Sunday nights during which drunk bartenders takes off their clothes and wrecks fire engines.

He gestured toward the smoking ruins of the firehouse.

I shrugged.

Rube said this town's baseball team is solid left-handed.

He said the citizens worship a guy what massacred a dozen men and the cemetery owner ain't buried nobody in fifty years.

I said okay where are we?

Rube said son don't you get the drift?

I shook my head.

Rube leaned toward me.

His voice was hoarse with horror.

He said why boy we is in Hell!

I grinned.

Rube said you know what part really locked it in?

He said Hell got to be the only place where a feller could get saddled with a hunnert-percent left-handed ball club.

We watched Moose meander across the street.

Moose said there is something supposed to happen today only I forgot what.

Rube said we got a ball game.

Moose said that's right.

He said Rube you sure got a good whatchacallit.

Rube said memory.

Moose said see there?

He said you just proved it.

Moose sat on the bench with us.

He said did we eat breakfast yet?

Rube said are you hungry?

Moose said you better believe it.

Rube said then we ain't ate breakfast yet.

I said Rube why don't you chuck this baseball thing and get married?

Rube said I'm so busy running from Tillie Zilch I don't got time to get married.

Moose said I wonder how long it takes a man to starve to death.

I said it's never too late Rube.

Rube said the hell it ain't.

He said getting married is for young fokes.

He said all there is for old fokes is being lonely.

He picked up a pebble and flipped it at an oak tree.

I caught the glimmer of a tear on his leathery cheek.

Rube said son you don't know the first thing about being lonely.

Moose said well maybe he don't know nothing about being lonely but I could write a book about being hungry.

...a umpire is a thoroughly honest man what nobody on earth trusts...

Monroe D. Underwood

We stood at the clubhouse door where Rube checked off the names of the arriving athletes.

Gaylord Messerschmitt was the last to show.

The wooden-legged catcher carried a small black satchel.

Rube said whatcha got in the satchel?

Moose said he probly got a bomb to blow up that catchers' convention he was talking about.

Gaylord Messerschmitt's piercing gray-green eyes lit up like neon signs.

He said that's right.

He said I built it myself.

He said I got the plans out of the *Christian Science Monitor.*

Rube grinned and winked at Gaylord Messerschmitt.

He said that's all right son.

He said just so's you ain't doing nothing dangerous.

The Creepy Hollow Vampires were taking batting practice when Tillie Zilch waved from her box seat behind the third base dugout.

As we approached her she made a neat backhand stab of a looping foul ball.

Rube nudged me.

He said if Tillie could hit the curve ball I'd have her in there this afternoon.

Tillie threw the ball to Rube.

She said that's fifty-two-thirty-two.

Rube nodded and wrote on the ball.

He tossed it back to Tillie and she dropped it into her purse without looking at it.

She said it's always the same old stuff.

Attila Honeywell trotted up.

He said that first base area sounds all hollow like a goddam bass drum.

He said them big black ants is up to something.

Rube said son how come them big black ants don't never bother nobody but you?

Attila Honeywell said I been wondering about that myself.

Five minutes before game time I spotted Brandy sitting near first base.

She smiled and licked her lips slowly.

We settled into the dugout and Rube sent Moose to home plate with the Stranger City lineup.

When Moose returned he said the ump just throwed me out of the game.

Rube said the goddam game ain't even started yet so how could he throw you out of it?

Moose said all I done was ask if he wanted me to read the lineup to him.

Rube said well put on another shirt and he'll think you're somebody else.

When Timothy Glumphwick strode to the pitcher's mound there were fifty-seven people in the park.

Including both teams.

The only customers were Tillie and Brandy and Brayfuss and Gilda Fitzhugh.

I said isn't somebody going to sing the national anthem?

Rube said what for?

He said there ain't nobody here to listen to it.

The big home plate umpire raised his arms.

In a booming voice he said I do hereby proclaim this to be the appropriate ripping moment for this ripping athletic contest to begin.

Rube stared at me.

He said anyplace else I ever been they just say play ball.

He said which serves to strengthen my contention that this ain't like anyplace else I ever been.

Timothy Glumphwick's first three pitches tore smoking holes in the backstop screen.

The fourth pitch hit the Creepy Hollow leadoff man on the leg and he was transported to first base on a stretcher.

Glumphwick nailed the second batter in the ribs.

This resulted in the second batter rolling on the ground and foaming at the mouth for several minutes.

Glumphwick clobbered the third Creepy Hollow hitter on the shoulder thereby bowling over Gaylord Messerschmitt and the home plate umpire.

Rube said get the derrick Moose.

He said he'll bust the next guy in the head and we'll all go up for murder.

Moose hiked out to the mound.

He was there for several minutes.

He returned without Timothy Glumphwick.

He said Glumphwick ain't coming out.

Rube said who says he ain't coming out?

Moose said Glumphwick.

Rube sighed.

He glanced down at Count Frazzlewitz.

The Count had just polished off a brace of Louisville Sluggers.

Rube spoke briefly and The Count bounded onto the playing field.

In a moment he had Glumphwick by the seat of his baseball knickers and the pitcher was dragged kicking and screaming into the dugout.

Rube gave him a reproachful look.

He said son in case you don't know who is running this here baseball team it just happens to be me.

Unexpected Kittzenwolf was summoned from the bullpen.

He was a dark-browed glowering man who had enjoyed a cup of coffee with Brooklyn during the war.

He was in the middle of a pitcher's nightmare.

Bases loaded and nobody out.

Kittzenwolf picked up the resin bag.

He glared at the runner on third base.

The runner took a long leadoff.

He danced around.

He waved his arms.

He was inviting a throw.

He got one.

It sailed high over third baseman Isoroku Yabuki's head and into the seats.

The runner on third base grinned with delight.

He jogged toward home plate.

Unexpected Kittzenwolf's throw to Gaylord Messerschmitt cut him down by twenty feet.

Unexpected Kittzenwolf had heaved the resin bag into the seats.

He had kept the baseball.

The home plate umpire made a violent motion with his right fist.

He roared this ripping runner is out.

The third base umpire raced to the plate.

He said this runner is not out.

He said the throwing of resin bags is illegal.

He said furthermore it is a great waste of resin.

The home plate umpire put his hands on his hips.

He said perhaps you have neglected to notice that I am the ripping umpire-in-chief.

He said I am the ripping master of all I survey.

He said I am as God.

The third base umpire said you are drunk with power.

The home plate umpire said you are out of this ripping ball game.

The third base umpire said you can't throw me out of the game.

He said I am the third base umpire.

The home plate umpire said I don't give a rip if you are the lord ripping mayor of ripping London you are out of this ripping ball game.

The third base umpire said how would you like to go rip yourself?

There was a threatening rumbling sound and the entire first base area caved in.

Attila Honeywell plummeted into the depths of the big black ant colony.

Timothy Glumphwick said well them big black ants got ole Attila Honeywell at last.

Moose said yes but what do they want with him?

Timothy Glumphwick said maybe they need a first baseman.

Moose said well that may be very true but it still don't explain what they want with Attila Honeywell.

While Attila Honeywell was being dragged to safety the home plate umpire raised his arms.

He said by the ripping power vested in me as ripping umpire-in-chief I do hereby declare this ripping ball game called off.

The four customers began to leave.

Rube sat motionless on the bench.

His elbows were on his knees and his head was in his hands.

I said are you all right Rube?

Rube looked up.

He said son I think there is something wrong here but I can't quite put my finger on it.

We heard the shurff's Model A pass the ball park.

The notes of the ancient barrel organ danced goldensweet through the June afternoon.

Rube looked at Moose.

He said don't say it.

Moose said I wasn't going to say nothing Rube.

He said I was just wondering what's the name of that tune.

40

> …I am probly the only man what receives get-sick cards…
>
> *Monroe D. Underwood*

When we came into the hotel the desk clerk said them Bobby Crackers Blitzkrieg for Christ trucks been rolling into town all afternoon.

He said must of been twenny-five or more.

He said you fellows going to attend?

Rube said well that would depend on whether there is anything else to attend.

The desk clerk said you could go to the possum races over at the bowling house.

Moose said hey Rube that sounds like a hell of a evening.

The desk clerk said watch out for that possum on alley five.

He said he goes out winging.

Rube said by God I can't hardly wait to attend that Bobby Crackers Blitzkrieg for Christ.

The desk clerk said oh just a minute Mr. Mountainstill.

He handed Rube a large white envelope.

He said that lady with the pretty eyes left it for you.

Rube opened the envelope and took out a card.

He looked at it and passed it to me.

It was beautiful.

It showed the silhouettes of a man and woman walking hand-in-hand into the sunset.

On the bottom in smooth flowing script was Rube I Love You.

It was signed Tillie.

Rube said maybe that will give you a idea of what I been up agin.

He said son have you ever heard of a war of attrition?

I shrugged.

I said somewhere.

Rube said well there comes a time when a army just ain't got nothing left to fight with.

Rube climbed the stairs slowly.

The way old men climb stairs.

The white handkerchief hanging from his hip pocket flopped back and forth.

Almost like a flag of surrender.

41

…a unusual moment is just a usual moment what went berserk…

Monroe D. Underwood

I stood by the rear window smoking a swaybacked Camel.

Brandy paced the floor.

She was all business now.

Her liquid brown eyes flashed excitedly.

She said Purdue tonight the chickens will come home to roost.

I said I thought they came home this afternoon.

Brandy smiled.

She said oh I enjoyed that immensely.

She said it was brief but it was simply brimming with unusual moments.

I said one of which was seeing you with your clothes on.

Brandy said sorry about that.

She said I'll be at the Blitzkrieg for Christ tonight but

don't look for me.

She said I'll catch up with you later.

I said when do you want to type my report to Chericola?

Brandy said tomorrow.

She said have you decided just how you'll do it?

I shrugged.

I said I'll make it like a letter.

I said I'll just say Dear Cool Lips and give him the whole shot.

I said this franchise isn't worth five cents and I'm going to tell him so.

I said the guy who sold it to him will probably wind up in a Pontiac trunk.

I said Chericola won't take this lying down.

Brandy snapped her fingers.

She said speaking of lying down.

> ...Impotency is no longer being able to do what you probly had no goddam business doing in the first place...
>
> *Monroe D. Underwood*

The Bobby Crackers Blitzkrieg for Christ had moved into a field at the extreme south end of Stranger City.

We arrived at twilight and it was a sight to behold.

The huge main tent was festooned with thousands of light bulbs of every imaginable color.

On its center pole a gigantic golden cross was illuminated by floodlights.

Tiny red and white striped tents dotted the grassy field.

There was something medieval about it all.

I half-expected to see Ivanhoe ride by.

We wandered among the little tents.

Here was the Italian sausage tent with fat sausages sputtering and smoking over a fiery bed of charcoal.

There was the hot dog tent with pink frankfurters cavorting playfully in a great caldron of boiling water.

We saw an ice cream tent and a lemonade tent and a popcorn tent.

We saw a tent where bumper stickers and pennants were sold.

I looked at the pennants.

Bobby Crackers Blitzkrieg for Christ.

I Love Bobby Crackers and God.

The Devil Is Afraid of Bobby Crackers.

The bumper stickers were of the glow-in-the-dark variety.

Jesus Saves.

Jesus Answers Prayer.

God Is Love.

Honk If You Love Bobby Crackers.

We stopped at the Bible tent.

We saw big white Bibles and little black Bibles and medium-sized brown Bibles.

We saw gold Bibles and purple Bibles and leopard-spotted Bibles.

We saw a Bobby Fire Crackers Bible.

It was done in red plastic and it was guaranteed by Bobby Crackers to wake somebody up.

We saw The Bible As It Should Have Been Written in the First Place.

The Bible As It Should Have Been Written in the First Place had been written by Bobby Crackers.

We came to a tent that sold Bobby Crackers songbooks and Bobby Crackers sheet music and Bobby Crackers recordings.

Another tent sold Bobby Crackers dolls.

Rube grunted.

He said you wind one up and it takes up a collection.

Moose said hey Rube this is just like a carnival.

He said I wonder do they got a Bobby Crackers roulette wheel.

Rube said well right about now it wouldn't surprise me if they had Bobby Crackers belly dancers.

We passed the Bobby Crackers shooting gallery where people blazed away at little red devils.

We passed the Bobby Crackers Ferris wheel with its sign that said Get Closer to God.

We passed the Bobby Crackers roulette wheel.

We entered the main tent.

Its floor was ankle-deep in fresh sawdust.

A sea of wooden benches sprawled in a vast half-moon to the foot of the blue velvet draped stage.

We found seats in the middle of the tent and Count Frazzlewitz snuggled down and got busy on a bench leg.

There was charged expectancy in the air and every seat was filled fifteen minutes before meeting time.

Moose said hey Rube this here Blitzkrieg drawed more people than the ball game.

Rube said yeah but we got the best show.

He said we got Attila Honeywell and his big black ant act.

A gentle breeze wafted the smells of food through the tent.

Women chattered and giggled and men pawed nervously through paperback hymnals.

There was the incessant howl of unhappy babies.

Moose said babies is always unhappy at revival meetings.

He said there got to be a reason.

Rube said of course there is a reason.

He said happy babies is barred from revival meetings.

He said they is carefully screened.

He said I think the CIA handles the whole business.

Moose said them unions is getting into everything.

Suddenly a bouncy bubbly man came dashing onto the stage.

He was followed by a group of big fellows that fanned out to take positions at pianos and organs and drums and several stringed instruments.

The bouncy bubbly man yelled hey let's hear it for Jesus.

A great roar went up.

He hollered my name is Biff Digby and I am God's anointed minstrel.

Another great roar went up.

Biff Digby hollered let's sing one for Jesus.

He led the crowd in singing "For He's a Jolly Good Fellow."

Following several "Jolly Good Fellows" Biff Digby had the crowd stand and sing "Precious Memories" and "Jesus on the Mainline."

A collection was taken up for the Bobby Crackers Society for Stamping Out Sin and Gin and Other Evils Too Numerous To Mention.

I threw a dollar into the basket and so did Moose.

Rube didn't contribute.

Biff Digby ordered us to turn and shake hands with the persons seated behind us.

I shook hands with Doctor Burnham and Rube shook hands with Cemetery Carson.

Moose grabbed the hand of a man who was eating a black walnut ice cream cone.

It was a very squishy handshake.

Moose muttered a few things about people who eat ice cream cones in church.

An usher came over and told Moose it was much too early to be speaking in tongues.

He mentioned that Moose could register for the tongues-speaking contest if he so desired.

Biff Digby introduced Yukon the Saved and Sanctified Seal and his Golden Gospel Fluegelhorn.

Yukon came flopping onto the stage.

Moose said hey Rube I bet he was easy to baptize.

Yukon devoured a bushel of fish and climbed a short ladder to which was attached a fluegelhorn.

He took a whack at "The Hallelujah Chorus" and he followed that with "If I Could Hear My Mother Pray Again."

As the notes of the fluegelhorn died away I said Rube there isn't a dry handkerchief left in the house.

Rube said yeah I think Moose borrowed them all to get that ice cream off his hands.

A collection was taken up for the Bobby Crackers Society for the Preservation of That Good Old Time Religion.

Moose and I pitched in dollar bills.

Rube didn't move a muscle.

During the taking of the collection Biff Digby told the congregation that Bobby Crackers would pray for anybody who had an ailment and fifty dollars.

He said that this offer did not include sexually impotent males.

Doctor Burnham leaned forward and said are any of you gentlemen impotent?

Moose said not me.

He said I'm Edwards.

Doctor Burnham said I have discovered a sure cure for impotency.

He said her name is Frieda Foster.

He said thirty bucks cheaper than Bobby Crackers.

An usher stopped by to tell Doctor Burnham that it was much too early to be speaking in tongues.

Biff Digby proclaimed that Georgie B. Belleau would sing "Rocked in the Cradle of the Deep."

A robed choir hummed an introduction and a big man appeared.

His hair was hanging in his eyes and he kept trying to adjust his horn-rimmed spectacles.

I said it looks like Georgie B. Belleau is wearing his glasses upside down.

Doctor Burnham leaned forward and said I saw that very fellow come out of Frieda Foster's place just half an hour ago.

Rube said he must of been in a hurry.

Doctor Burnham said yeah because he's wearing Frieda's wig.

Georgie B. Belleau cut loose with a basso profundo.

Within moments the tent was full of Ike Kelton's cows.

While order was being restored two more collections were taken up.

Moose and I tossed half-dollars into each basket.

Rube yawned.

Now Biff Digby smiled broadly and said we have an extra-special treat for you good people of Stranger City.

He said it is with extreme pride that we present the Bobby Crackers Belly Dancers.

He said the girls are gonna shake it for Jesus.

The lights dimmed and three scantily attired fat women waddled out and began to shake it for Jesus.

Moose couldn't get over the size of the crowd.

He said hey Rube I can't get over the size of the crowd.

He said damn near everybody is here.

Rube said yep damn near everybody but God.

The Bobby Crackers Belly Dancers were warmly applauded.

Biff Digby said folks it just keeps getting better all the time.

He said with us tonight is the world's foremost female gospel singer.

He said let's have a great big hand for Sister Lucy Halfbright.

Sister Lucy Halfbright came swishing to the microphone.

She was a pale scrawny woman with the nose of a kingfisher and the fangs of a cornered mountain lion.

She wore a flowing blue robe with a pair of large white cardboard wings attached to the shoulders.

She carried a Bible in one hand and a parking violation ticket in the other.

She gave a lengthy talk about godlessness in the Powersville Police Department.

Then she mentioned that several Christians had been late for the six o'clock prayer wheel.

She said that God had told her that He had better things to do than just sit around waiting for tardy prayer wheel members to show up.

She said that she was about to favor the audience with a song of her own composing entitled "The Lord Lifted Me Up to a High and Holy Place from Which I Sit in Constant Righteous Judgment on My Sinful Neighbors."

Rube said if the verse is half as long as the title eternity will be over afore she gets to the chorus.

The robed choir warbled a chord and Sister Lucy Halfbright rared back and let fly.

Several women's hats flew off.

A few people broke out in rashes.

Half a dozen children went into convulsions.

Count Frazzlewitz began to howl brokenheartedly.

Moose said hey Rube is this Halfbright broad a contralto?

Rube said no she is a fartralto.

When Sister Lucy Halfbright was finished another collection was taken up.

Biff Digby announced that this collection was for the express purpose of transporting Sister Lucy Halfbright and her glorious message in song to sin-crushed Upper Maroovia.

The basket was passed.

Rube contributed forty-six dollars and eleven cents.

He threw in his pocketknife and his comb and three cigars.

He added his Zippo lighter and his Masonic ring and three sticks of spearmint chewing gum.

He topped his offering with an IOU for thirty-nine million dollars.

He looked at me.

He said son let me tell you a feller don't get a chance like this every day.

Fifteen uniformed trumpeters stepped from behind the blue velvet backdrop.

They blew a fanfare that lasted ten minutes.

The great moment was upon us.

Bobby Crackers appeared.

An ear-busting wave of sound rocketed into the Stranger City night.

Fifteen women fainted on the spot and ushers restrained countless others who were attempting to disrobe.

Bobby Crackers was an angelically handsome man with wavy blonde hair and enormous innocent blue eyes.

He wore a hand-tailored suit of pale gold satin on which

thousands of tiny blue crosses had been embroidered.

He smiled a capped-toothed smile.

He held up a pink-palmed hand and said peace be still.

The waves subsided.

Count Frazzlewitz growled low in his throat.

Bobby Crackers said can you say amen?

The amen must have rattled windows in Buckingham Palace.

Bobby Crackers got right at it.

He said that Stranger City was on God's hit list.

He said that Stranger City was steeped in sin and everybody in it was going to hell if they didn't straighten out.

He said that there was too much drinking in Stranger City.

He said that whiskey was a killer.

Rube said well he's sure right about that.

He said I had a uncle what tripped over a case of Old Rimrock and busted his neck.

An usher came along and told Rube it was much too early to be speaking in tongues.

Bobby Crackers said he knew of a Stranger City man who kept a bottle of whiskey hidden in his garage.

He said that this man's neighbor was always sneaking over to steal drinks.

Instantly five separate fistfights broke out and the ushers were hard pressed to subdue the participants.

Bobby Crackers said that Stranger City was a hotbed of indiscriminate sexual activity.

He said he knew of a Stranger City woman who sold her body for twenty dollars.

He said that this woman had a terrible sexual disease known as Medusa's Revenge.

In the twinkling of an eye a dozen men leaped to their feet and raced from the tent in the direction of Doctor Burnham's office.

As they faded from sight Doctor Burnham was leading the field and Georgie B. Belleau was closing fast on the outside.

Bobby Crackers went on and on.

He discussed gambling and motion pictures and the wearing of lipstick.

Also short skirts and tobacco and popular music.

He said these were instruments of the Devil.

He called down a curse on those who didn't contribute to the Lord's work.

Then he called down a curse upon those who *did* contribute to the Lord's work.

He said they didn't contribute enough.

Bobby Crackers romped and stomped.

He ripped and snorted.

He laughed and he cried.

He jumped up and down and he waved his Bible in the air.

He mentioned that the same Bible was available at the Bible tent and that it was marked down to fifty-nine ninety-five.

He added that hot dogs would be reduced in price after the service.

He called on all of Stranger City to join him in his glorious campaign for Jesus.

He announced an altar call.

The robed choir sang "Will the Circle be Unbroken?"

Bobby Crackers began to weep uncontrollably.

He told of the death of his mother and how he would meet her in the sky and he said that pennants and bumper stickers were now being sold at half price.

The choir switched to "Just As I Am."

Hundreds of people began to stream down the sawdust trail to the altar.

Rube said let's get out of here before God wipes this abscess from the face of the earth.

When we were out of the tent Moose said aw Rube I wanted to stay for the tongues-speaking contest.

Rube said Moose you see one tongues-speaking contest you seen them all.

Moose said yeah but I ain't seen my first one yet.

Rube looked around.

He said where the hell is Count Frazzlewitz?

He started back into the tent.

I grabbed him by the arm.

I pointed to the illuminated cross on the center pole of the tent.

It was listing.

And listing.

The center pole snapped with the sound of a hand grenade explosion.

The big tent collapsed with a great whooshing puff of hot air.

Rube shook his head.

He said Count Frazzlewitz strikes again.

In the white glare of the floodlights the scene was unreal.

The broad expanse of canvas rolled and billowed like a stormy winter sea.

Men cursed and women screamed.

We could hear the impassioned voice of Bobby Crackers imploring the immediate intercession of the Almighty.

One corner of the tent flopped briefly and Count

Frazzlewitz appeared.

He was accompanied by Yukon the Saved and Sanctified Seal.

Yukon was dragging his fluegelhorned ladder.

He headed for Darby's Jump Off.

Count Frazzlewitz bounced smilingly up to Rube.

He was carrying a large swatch of pale gold satin embroidered with tiny blue crosses.

Rube patted The Count on the head.

He said *du bist ein gut hund.*

Moose said hey Rube I never knowed you could speak in tongues.

43

> ...religion is something what lets you keep right on doing what you never stopped doing only you can't brag about it no more...
>
> *Monroe D. Underwood*

By midnight Stranger City was up for grabs.

The populace was crocked on religion.

There was a prayer meeting on every street corner.

There was much speaking in tongues.

Hymns were sung and the music poured through the open windows.

Brandy said Purdue don't stop now.

I said I got to stop now.

I said there is absolutely no way I can accomplish this to the strains of "Take Up Thy Cross and Follow Me."

Brandy said I have an idea.

She said let's take a blanket and go up to Darby's Jump Off.

She said it's quiet there and we can do it all night.

I rolled over and sat on the edge of the bed.

I looked at the floor.

I said oh God our help in ages past.

I said oh God who set the suffering captives free.

I said blessed Savior still our refuge.

Brandy sat up.

She said Purdue things didn't go too well tonight.

She said in fact the whole evening was a bust.

She said now if you're going to get religion you're just going to have to wait until tomorrow morning.

She said that's an order.

44

...the difference between discriminate sex and indiscriminate sex ain't worth going into...

Monroe D. Underwood

The clock in the lobby said twelve-thirty.

The desk clerk looked at it and then at me.

He threw a wary glance at the lobby doorway.

He said they've gone bananas out there.

He said I ain't slept wink number goddam one.

I said same here.

I said of course it's mighty hot in my room.

The desk clerk said things was a whole lot better when we didn't have nothing going on but drinking and indiscriminate sex.

He said hey by the way I'd sure like to have me some indiscriminate sex with that gal in 208.

I said who's that?

The desk clerk checked the register.

He said Miss Brandy Alexander.

He said have you seen her?

I shrugged.

I said yeah now and then.

The desk clerk said just give me one shot at that.

He said I'll wear the little rascal out.

I said I think that's what Goliath said.

The desk clerk said who?

I said Goliath.

The desk clerk looked at the register.

He said he ain't checked in yet.

I stretched on the davenport and tried to sleep.

The blast nearly blew me onto the floor.

It had come from the south.

I stumbled out onto Stranger Avenue.

An evil-looking pillar of gray swirling smoke obliterated the south end of town.

A woman was screaming Come Thou Almighty King.

An old man grabbed my arm.

He yelled pray brother it's the end of the world.

The shurff's Ford went by with its barrel organ chirping.

I watched it vanish into the smoke.

Brandy appeared at my side in robe and scuffs.

She said Purdue what the hell's happening down here?

I shrugged.

I said it's something up by the ball park.

A sudden silence had shrouded Stranger City.

We shuffled around in the dust and waited.

Brandy said I thought you were just going to the lobby for cigarettes.

I said yeah but I got to talking to the desk clerk.

The shurff's car emerged from the thinning smoke.

Like the Flying Dutchman from a fogbank.

I waved to him.

He stopped.

I said what was it?

The shurff said somebody must of planted a bomb in the baseball clubhouse.

I said have you seen Gaylord Messerschmitt?

The shurff said if you mean that wooden-legged catcher he got religion and left town.

He said he claimed that God had called him to the ministry.

I said I think maybe he forgot something.

The shurff drove away.

Brandy said Purdue let's go to bed.

I said look why don't we just go over to the park bench?

Brandy frowned.

She said well it might be just a bit cramped.

She said but it's a challenge.

She squeezed my arm.

She said come on.

She said I'm game if you are.

45

> …in Illinois you got to be able to prove adultery before you can buy a drink…
>
> *Monroe D. Underwood*

The phone rang at eight ayem.

Brandy yawned and purred deliciously.

She kissed my shoulder.

She said Purdue answer that damned thing will you?

She said it rang all night and there was nobody on the line.

She said didn't you hear it?

I said Brandy last night I could have slept through a naval bombardment.

Rube was on the phone.

He said can you come down to the lobby?

He said the manure has just hit the fan.

I hung up and got dressed.

Brandy said hurry back.

She said we have to make up for lost time.

I said what lost time?

Brandy said what do you mean what lost time?

She said my God I didn't see you for six months.

I stumbled down the stairs and into the lobby.

Rube and Moose were seated on the davenport.

The Stranger City baseball team stood clustered in front of them.

All but Gaylord Messerschmitt.

Rube said we got us a problem.

I lit a fractured Camel and sat next to him.

Rube looked up at Opus Ganderneck.

He said will you repeat your statement for the benefit of Mr. Purdue?

Opus Ganderneck rolled his eyes upward.

He placed his left hand over his heart.

He raised his right hand high above his head.

Rube said just the statement if you will please.

Opus Ganderneck said we are quitting baseball because it is a sinful game with personal gain at its root.

Dudley Shift said not to mention greed.

Isoroku Yabuki sang "Grory Grory Harrerujah."

Attila Honeywell tapped Opus Ganderneck on the shoulder.

He said don't forget the part about them big black ants.

Horsefish Hallahan said farewell oh dark and dismal past.

Barnaby Klutz said onward and upward.

Isoroku Yabuki sang "Ret the Rower Rights be Burning."

Sorehead Hawkins said I feel the joy-bells deep in my gut.

Rube nudged me.

He said wait till he feels my shoe deep in his drawers.

Isoroku Yabuki sang "This Ritter Right of Mine."

Timothy Glumphwick said yea though I walk through

the valley I shall not commit adultery.

Horsefish Hallahan said you got that all wrong.

Unexpected Kittzenwolf said leave the kid alone.

He said if he don't want to commit adultery in the valley that is his business.

Isoroku Yabuki sang "Reaning on the Everrasting Arms."

We watched as the Stranger City Strangers turned to file out of the lobby.

Isoroku Yabuki led them in singing "Ruvv Rifted Me."

When they were gone Moose said hey Rube that Barnaby Klutz sure sings a lousy tenor.

46

...bumper stickers is things what horses' asses sticks on the asses of automobiles...

Monroe D. Underwood

We were in the lounge of the Stranger City Hotel at noon.

I was spending the final minutes with Rube and Moose.

The shurff was to drive them over to Raccoon Rapids for the two o'clock bus.

I said Rube I'm going to miss you guys.

I said I really mean that.

Rube said son I know you do.

I said I guess you'll be changing buses in Chicago.

Rube said yeah we got a two-hour layover.

I handed Rube the envelope containing my report to Cool Lips Chericola.

I said would you deliver this for me?

I said this guy got offices on Randolph Street right next door to the bus terminal.

I said Shadyside Enterprises.

Rube nodded.

He said I'll have Moose handle it.

He said I'll be so glad to get out of this crazy town I won't know Randolph Street from the Black Hole of Calcutta.

Moose said hey Rube this is a swell town.

He said I had me a real good time here.

Rube said Moose you would probly have a real good time at the Spanish Inquisition.

Moose said I missed that one but I seen "The French Erection" over in Richwood.

Eddie Gee slammed a farewell round of drinks onto the bar.

We downed them and walked to the park bench.

Gilda Fitzhugh was waiting.

She said oh Mr. Mountainstill would you do me a favor and give this to Editor Sam Cohen at the Chicago *Globe*?

She pushed an envelope at Rube.

She said tell him it's from Gilda.

She said the *Globe* is just around the corner from the bus depot.

Rube said Moose will take care of it.

He said Moose used to be a mailman.

Gilda Fitzhugh went away.

Rube said I was afraid to say no.

He said she might have stepped on me.

He put one foot up on his mile-weary old suitcase.

He said well Moose and me got out of here undefeated and we never done that good afore.

There was a sadness in his voice.

I slapped Rube's bony shoulder.

I said Rube nobody will ever beat you guys.

Rube said I'm going back to Greenbrier County.

He looked down at his scuffed brown shoes and white socks.

He said I'm gonna sit on my front porch and listen to them crickets say stay home you goddam fool stay home.

We heard the barrel organ approaching.

Moose said that's sure a purty song.

Rube said please Moose not now.

The shurff pulled up and Rube began to look around.

He said I kind of figgered Tillie Zilch might drop by.

They stuffed Count Frazzlewitz and the suitcases into the rear with the barrel organ compressor.

Rube and Moose sat up front with the shurff.

I said Rube how are you ever going to get that dog on a bus?

Rube took out a pair of dark glasses and put them on.

He said I always tell the driver I'm blind.

He reached out and grabbed my hand with his clean hard grip.

He said that's probly not so far from the truth anyway.

I said so long boys.

Rube said good-bye son and may God bless you.

The little blue car pulled away with its barrel organ hammering out its eternal melody.

The music dwindled and died.

I dried my eyes and started across the street to the hotel.

A rusted-out black Chrysler came fishtailing in my direction.

There was an enormous cloud of Stranger City dust in its wake.

The crazed vehicle skidded to a stop.

Tillie Zilch leaned out and yelled which way did he go?

I pointed toward Raccoon Rapids.

Tillie said how much start does he have?

I said maybe thirty seconds.

I said it'll be easy.

I said it's only six miles and his bus doesn't leave until two

Tillie's violet eyes were shining.

She said come here for a second.

I walked to the side of the beat-up Chrysler.

The backseat was full of suitcases.

Tillie was holding a baseball.

She said look at this.

It was inscribed 5,232 To Tillie With Love From Rube.

Tillie pressed it to her breast.

Tears gushed down her cheeks.

Her voice was like a faint busted bagpipe.

She said I just noticed it fifteen minutes ago.

She threw a trembling headlock on me.

She kissed me ferociously.

She said I'm going to send you something.

She said I know you helped me.

The Chrysler departed amid flying pebbles and burning rubber smoke.

On its crumpled bumper was a sticker from the Bobby Crackers Blitzkrieg for Christ.

Jesus Answers Prayer.

47

> ...youth ain't nothing but a shortcut to old age...
>
> *Monroe D. Underwood*

Brandy was packing my things.

Very slowly.

She said Purdue we've had four days of undiluted heaven.

She said haven't we?

I shrugged.

I said oh sure.

I said a couple times I was only inches from the pearly gates.

Brandy kissed me.

She said Purdue you say such nice things.

I said I should have been a diplomat.

Brandy said I can't find your report to Chericola.

I said Moose is going to deliver it.

I said Chericola's offices are next door to the bus terminal.

Brandy said oh that's right.

I said Gilda Fitzhugh gave him her baseball article to

take to the Chicago *Globe*.

Brandy said yes the Fitzhughs own stock in the *Globe*.

She said I've seen some of Gilda's stuff.

She said it all comes out sounding like "Hiawatha."

She said this is Chance and this is Brandy in the town of Stranger City where they make mad love at midnight in the town of Stranger City.

She said like that.

She said do you want more?

I said not really.

There was a knock on the door.

I opened it and the shurff walked in.

He said I reckoned I ought to come by and shake hands and say so long and things like that.

I said thanks shurff.

The shurff said when I leave here I got to go arrest ole Horatio Brayfuss.

Brandy's head snapped up.

She said whatever on earth for?

The shurff said fer perferating a fraud.

Brandy said how do you mean?

The shurff said ole Brayfuss tole everybody he buried them bad guys under the baseball clubhouse.

He said that explosion blowed a hole more than eight foot deep.

He said I been all over that piece of ground with a fine-tooth comb and there wasn't no bones nor no belt buckles nor no guns nor no bullets nor no nothing.

Brandy said shurff it goes a step beyond that.

She said there was no Stranger either.

The shurff said I think maybe I figgered that out already.

Brandy said you can't arrest Brayfuss.

The shurff bristled.

He said I'm the shurff ain't I?

He said hoaxes is illegal ain't they?

Brandy said yes shurff but you're up against the seven year statute.

The shurff said seven years my foot.

He said why that goofy statute been up on the hill fer going on fifty.

Brandy closed my suitcase and took the shurff's hand.

She said shurff The Stranger wasn't an evil bit of trickery.

She said he was a publicity stunt.

She said he drew attention to Stranger City and he gave its people something to be proud of.

She said he has become an inspirational legend.

She said don't the children of Stranger City sing "Hooray for The Stranger" in music classes?

She said doesn't the Stranger City High School football team take the field to "Hail to The Stranger"?

The shurff said don't help 'em much.

He said last year we lost ten straight.

He said Powersville beat us a hunnert and twelve to nothing.

Brandy said that doesn't really matter.

She said the people of this community have always looked up to The Stranger.

The shurff said well we had to.

He said that damn statute got to be nigh twenny foot high.

Brandy said shurff would you destroy all of that wonderful tradition?

The shurff kicked at my throw rug.

He said well I reckon not.

I shook the shurff's hand and told him so long.

Brandy kissed his wrinkled cheek.

We heard him go down the stairs.

We heard his car go down the street with its barrel organ tinkling.

Brandy sat on the bed with tears on her face.

She said there's something about elderly gentlemen.

She said they destroy me.

I thought of Tillie Zilch and found a lump in my throat.

I said those old ladies are no pushovers either.

48

...a balalaika is something what if you can't play it don't worry about it...

Monroe D. Underwood

Brandy looked up with misery in her liquid brown eyes.

She said Purdue I've failed my country.

She said this is the first case I've ever blown.

I said I don't know what you're talking about but welcome to the club.

Brandy said I had the bastards right in my clutches.

She said I had thirty special agents planted in the audience.

She said if the damned tent hadn't caved in I'd have that pair of America-hating sonsofbitches behind bars right now.

I said who?

Brandy said Bobby Crackers and Leonid Groganovitch.

I said I don't get it.

Brandy said didn't you recognize Groganovitch?

She said you remember him don't you?

I said sure but I didn't see him.

Brandy said Groganovitch was the big man who played the balalaika.

She said he has a crew cut now and his beard is gone.

I shrugged.

I said what's a balalaika?

Brandy tossed herself onto the bed.

She lit a pair of cigarettes and jammed one into my mouth.

She said let's start from the top.

She said Purdue the organization known as DADA is no longer funded by the Kremlin.

She said Russia's arms program has become so expensive that many of its pet subversive groups have been forced to find means of self-support.

She said it's a simple matter of a ruble shortage.

She said DADA made the conversion with its customary efficiency.

She said every dime that this hellish gang spends on the eventual overthrow of our government is contributed by well-meaning God-fearing Americans at the Bobby Crackers Blitzkrieg for Christ.

I said I don't get it.

Brandy said Bobby Crackers is really Boboi Krakezoff.

She said he's a top-echelon KGB agent assigned to DADA and he has spent years mastering the techniques of the hustlers in America's rural evangelistic field.

She said in addition to supplying DADA with operating capital his Blitzkrieg for Christ has served as dispatching headquarters for all the Soviet spies in the country.

She said they just attended services and took their instructions from the stage.

She said simplicity is the essence of beauty and let me tell you this was an exquisite operation.

I said how did it work?

Brandy said it always happened during the tongues-speaking contests.

She said Groganovitch appeared in every contest.

She said I haven't the foggiest notion what languages the other contestants employed but Groganovitch spoke in Russian.

She said he rolled his eyes and waved his arms and jumped around like the rest but when he opened his mouth it was to spout instructions to Russian operatives in the crowd.

I said how did you get onto it?

Brandy said Horatio Brayfuss is the CIA fieldman in this area.

She said he also owns the Stranger City Bank.

She said DADA has its account there.

I said my God don't tell me that they just walked in and opened an account under the name of Destroy America Destroy America.

Brandy said no they switched to Dental Association of Dillingham Alaska but when Brayfuss saw that the checks were signed by Bobby Crackers and cashed by people with names like Katkov and Pobedonostsev and Vyshnegredski he whistled up the hounds.

She said of which I am the head bitch.

I said what was the real tip-off?

Brandy said that goddam balalaika.

She said a balalaika simply doesn't belong in a gospel band.

I shrugged.

I said why not?

I said doesn't God like balalaikas?

Brandy said well perhaps it wasn't a total washout after all.

She said at least we've broken the back of the outfit.

She said they'll need a new gimmick now.

I said I don't see anything wrong with playing gospel music on a balalaika.

I said what the hell the notes are the same and everything.

Brandy said but I detest the thought of those two lizards running loose.

I said I doubt that the musical instrument is terribly important to God.

I said I think the thing that really counts is what's in your heart.

Brandy said I called Chicago and there's an all-points bulletin out but I'm afraid they've skipped the net.

I said you see if your heart is pure I don't think God would mind if you played gospel music on a kazoo.

Brandy said oh dear God Purdue will you shut up?

She said I'm in no mood for theological profundities.

I shrugged.

I said watch your language.

Brandy stood and began to remove her clothing.

She said pull down the shades and let's have one for the road.

> ...oncet I knowed a feller what busted a window and had seven seconds bad luck...his jugular vein got in the way...
>
> *Monroe D. Underwood*

I dropped the rear shade and went to the front window.

In the bright Stranger City sunlight I saw the shurff walking down the middle of Stranger Avenue.

He carried a double-barreled shotgun the size of a small cannon.

Ahead of him were two men.

They walked a trifle unsteadily.

One had a huge hole in the seat of his pants and the other carried a stringed musical instrument that had a triangular body.

I said Brandy come here and tell me if this is a balalaika.

50

…indecent exposure is a three-hunnertpound woman in a three-ounce swimming suit…

Monroe D. Underwood

The shurff was saying well I got one of ’em on a indecent exposure rap.

He said I got both of ’em for climbing The Stranger’s monument.

He said we don’t allow nobody on The Stranger’s monument.

He said what the hell The Stranger is a inspirational legend.

Brandy said what were they doing on The Stranger’s monument?

The shurff said they was trying to excape from some kind of animal what was just a-snapping at their asses.

He said never seen nothing like it.

He said it had funny-looking legs.

He ran a quivering hand through his white hair.

He said you fokes is looking at a man what is done took his last drink.

He said when I marched them looneys away I swear to God I heard music floating down the hill.

I said what sort of music?

The shurff said it sounded like a horn.

I said was it a tune you recognized?

The shurff nodded.

He said sure was.

He looked up.

Sheepishly.

He said but there wasn't nobody up there but that animal.

I said what was the tune?

The shurff said it was "America the Beautiful."

51

…trying harder don't never make it harder…

Monroe D. Underwood

Darkness had enveloped Stranger City.

The great butter-yellow moon wallowed through a sea of ragged clouds.

Brandy's Porsche moved silkily away from the hotel.

Brandy said will you come work with me?

I shrugged.

I said give me a chance to recover from this ordeal.

Brandy said ordeal?

I said well you know.

I said the baseball team and everything.

We turned beyond the ball park and Darby's Jump Off loomed blackly on our left.

Brandy eased the Porsche to a stop and looked.

She said next time we're here I want you to make love to me up there.

I said okay next time.

Brandy said shhhhhhhh.

She said Purdue listen.

She said what did you hear?

I said I heard you saying shhhhhhhh.

I said with eight h's.

Brandy said try harder.

I tried harder.

Down from Darby's Jump Off and across the chasm of ten thousand yesterdays drifted the silvery notes of a faraway horn.

They rode the balmy night breeze from Stranger City to eternity.

"America the Beautiful."

Brandy said oh Purdue I think that's wonderful.

She said what do you think?

I stroked the back of my neck where the hair stood straight up.

I said I think we better get back to Chicago.

52

> …oncet I knowed a man what put fifty piranhas in his bathtub…then his mother-in-law used the shower in the basement and spoilt everything…
>
> *Monroe D. Underwood*

I was parked on the couch with a 1936 *Eagles* magazine.

I was reading "Where Did All These Fokkers Come From?" by Arch Blockhouse.

I took a slug of my Old Washensachs beer.

I said it's good to be home.

Betsy said sweetheart it's wonderful to have you back.

She glanced at the enormous empty cardboard carton in the corner of our living room.

She said that was awfully nice of Tillie Zilch.

She said I think.

She said but what are we going to do with five thousand two hundred and thirty-one baseballs?

I shrugged.

Betsy said well we're certainly going to have to get them out of the bathtub.

She picked up a copy of the Chicago *Globe* and curled herself into our big blue chair.

She said I tried to call you in Stranger City.

She said a woman kept answering.

I shrugged.

I said probably the maid.

Betsy said at four in the morning?

I said anything can happen in Stranger City.

Betsy said the voice seemed vaguely familiar.

She said sort of soft and husky-sweet.

I said well Betsy I wouldn't dwell on it.

I said the maid's voice was sort of soft and husky-sweet as I recall.

I said she was a very old woman by the way.

Betsy said uh-huh.

I said what night did you call?

Betsy said Monday.

I said well that was when the clubhouse blew up.

I said in all the confusion they probably rang the wrong room.

Betsy said ten times?

I shrugged.

Betsy began to read her newspaper.

She giggled.

Then she laughed heartily.

She said oh my God.

She said Chance I'm reading about Stranger City.

She said the writing is represented as being some dumbbell's report to a mobster who owns a baseball team down there.

She said it's called "Dear Cool Lips."

She said now who could ever be called Cool Lips?

I shrugged.

Betsy said of course such crazy things could never happen and no one could possibly be this stupid.

She chuckled.

She said why there isn't even any punctuation.

I said well Betsy punctuation ain't exactly one of the Ten Commandments you know.

Betsy said just imagine catchers with wooden legs and firehouses burning down and dogs being sent out to relieve pitchers.

She said you simply have to read this.

I said who wrote it?

Betsy said let's see.

She said a woman named Gilda Fitzhugh.

She said it says here that she won a Lucas Award with it.

I said what's a Lucas Award?

Betsy said whatever it is it's worth five thousand dollars.

> …I got a uncle what lives in Upper Maroovia…he went on a visit and found out there was no way to get back…
>
> *Monroe D. Underwood*

Wallace was saying I am going to sell this house of horrors and move to the wilds of Upper Maroovia where I will hunt bxfpsts.

I said Wallace you better stay the hell out of Upper Maroovia.

Wallace said why?

He said bxfpsts ain't dangerous.

I said no but Sister Lucy Halfbright is.

Old Dad Underwood said I ain't never seen none of them creatures.

Wallace said they all looks the same.

He said they is delicious pan-fried.

Old Dad Underwood said well to each his own but I

ain't about to eat nothing I can't pronounce.

I lit a frazzled Camel and listened to the jukebox pla[illegible] *Alte Kameraden.*

Wallace bought me a beer.

He said how did it go in Stranger City?

I shrugged.

I said how much time you got?

Wallace glanced over my shoulder.

He said Chance that guy is back.

Cool Lips Chericola came in.

He was followed closely by Fat Ears Bonnoroni.

Fat Ears sat at the bar and Chericola took a seat in the third booth.

He lit a cigar and leaned back.

I picked up my beer and sat across from him.

Chericola slid a pair of one-thousand-dollar bills across the table.

He whipped out an envelope and opened it.

He said hey kid amma now reada you fromma you Stranger City report.

He cleared his throat.

He said inna valley of forever atta foota greena mountain olda clubhouse gone forever where the windsa moan with sorrow anna tree tops rustla softly inna shade and inna shadow witha dusta Stranger City velvet dusta Stranger City lay eternal onna lilacs inna sunlight anna moonlight witha dew drop anna tear drop listna to the barrela organ make sweet music inna valley inna valley of forever.

He said that's only firsta sentence.

Chericola leaned across the table and put his hand on my arm.

He squinted at me.

He said hey kid whattsa that mean?

I shrugged.

I said it means Moose Edwards blew it.

Chericola silenced me with a wave of his hand.

He said is sounda justa like "Hiawatha."

He said you know "Hiawatha"?

I shrugged.

I said not personally.

Chericola said hey kid is this Hiawatha who getta me kicked outta school.

An affectionate teardrop shone in Chericola's eye.

A tear from the mossy well of memory.

He brushed it away.

He said damn cigar smoke.

He said is reada "Hiawatha" inna matha class and inna gymma class.

He pulled out a handkerchief and blew his nose.

His voice quavered.

He said bya shoresa Gitchagoomba bya shina blue sea water stooda wiggawam Nakoma anna grandson Hiawatha.

He said hey kid you notta dumb as you look.

He said thissa beautifula stuff.

He said hey kid amma senda you bonus.

He said sixxa grand.

I didn't say anything.

Chericola dried his reptilian eyes.

His pockmarked face grew hard.

He said hey kid you read thatta Deara Coola Lipsa stuff inna paper?

I said no but I heard about it.

Chericola said hey kid broad whattsa write that gonna end up inna trunka Pontiac.

I shrugged.

I said I doubt if she'll fit.

54

…when I stop to remember
The good friends I've had
My very worst enemies
Don't seem quite so bad…

Monroe D. Underwood

I was halfway home when I thought of cigarettes.

I reached into a pocket of my coat.

Nothing.

I tried the other.

No cigarettes but I found a cassette.

I didn't recognize it as one of mine.

I stopped in front of a drugstore and bought a pack of Camels.

When I came out I lit one and popped the cassette into the player.

The barrel organ tune cavorted through the Olds.

Stranger City came back to me.

Its lilacs.

Its clear starry nights.

Its great butter-yellow moon.

Its out-of-tune piano.

Its bright dew-spangled mornings.

Its sun-warmed park bench.

Its hill and its grotesque monument and its thousand outraged birds.

Its silence.

Its dust.

The merry-melancholy tune bounced along and a voice came from the speakers.

A soft husky-sweet voice.

Brandy Alexander said Purdue I'll be seeing you.

I shrugged.

I turned the tape player off.

I started the Olds and drove west.

I couldn't think of a single reason to doubt her.

…I thought I saw a dragon up in my apple tree…I never mess with dragons and they don't mess with me…

Monroe D. Underwood

More from Ross H. Spencer

THE CHANCE PURDUE SERIES

THE DADA CAPER

Chance Purdue may be better at a lot of things than he is at detecting, but he's the only man for the job when the FBI comes looking for someone to take on the Soviet-inspired DADA conspiracy.

Plus, he needs a paycheck. Chance gets off to a rough start as he's led on a merry chase through Chicago's underbelly and drawn into a case of deception that can only be solved with the help of a mysterious femme fatale who's as beautiful as she is cunning.

THE REGGIS ARMS CAPER

Try as he may, Chance Purdue can't seem to escape the world of private investigation. The now tavern owner returns to action to protect Princess Sonia of Kaleski, who claims to be the wife of an old Army buddy. Convinced he'll get to the bottom of things at his Army battalion's reunion, Chance indulges in the entertainment while leaving the more serious detective work to his new colleague, the scintillating Brandy Alexander. For Chance, the case provides more fun than intrigue, and yet its solution is a surprise for everyone involved.

THE ABU WAHAB CAPER

What happens when Chicago detective Chance Purdue is hired to protect a gambler with a target on his head? For starters, all hell breaks loose…

"Bet-a-Bunch" Dugan is being hunted by International DADA (Destroy America, Destroy America) conspirators, a terrorist organization out for control of the world's oil market. Dugan needs more than a little luck to walk away unscathed. He needs a Chance, and though he knows that half of Purdue's reputation is that of a guy you are aching to punch, the other half is that he's a dogged, if occasionally doomed, investigator.

No matter where Purdue's leads take him, though, he always seems to be one step behind DADA. As a hapless Chance watches DADA's deadly scheme move forward, a siren named Brandy Alexander enters the picture and things finally fall into place, or so Chance hopes...

THE RADISH RIVER CAPER

Private Investigator Chance Purdue and Brandy Alexander work in tandem on a case that finds them traveling to the Illinois town of Radish River. The CIA continues to need help putting a stop to the DADA (Destroy America, Destroy America) Conspiracy, a terrorist organization whose latest plot is completely under wraps, except that it promises immense destruction. Things prove difficult for Chance and Brandy as they do what they can to remain focused on the task at hand. But it's hard when distractions from football-playing gorillas, chariot races, copious booze—and especially each other—weave in and out of their lives and keep this case on the back burner.

DEATH WORE GLOVES

When Sister Rosetta's niece goes missing, the nun (whose favorite poison is anything bottle-bound and boozy) hires shifty P.I. Tut Willow to find dear Gladys. But as Tut pulls back the curtain on Gladys' checkered past, he also finds that someone doesn't want her found, and soon bodies begin to pile up. Is Sister Rosetta, lured by a twisted sense of family loyalty, behind the deaths of those out to harm her niece, or are Tut and Gladys just pawns in a much darker game?

Full of laugh-out-loud comedy and the darkest of intrigue, the author of DEATH WORE GLOVES draws together femme fatales, a not-so-saintly nun, and a gumshoe willing to do anything to help an old flame.

KIRBY'S LAST CIRCUS

When the CIA chooses Birch Kirby, a mediocre detective with a personal life even less thrilling than his professional one, no one is more surprised by the selection than Birch himself. But the Agency needs someone for a secret mission, and Birch may be just the clown for the job. Going undercover as a circus performer, he travels to Grizzly Gulch to investigate the source of daily, un-decodeable secret messages that are being transmitted to the KGB. Birch interacts with wildly colorful characters while stumbling through performances as well as his assignment. With the clock ticking, Birch must hurry to take a right step toward bringing the curtain down on this very important case.

THE LACEY LOCKINGTON SERIES

THE FIFTH SCRIPT

Detective Lacey Lockington always gets the job done, but making the omelets of solved cases usually involves breaking a lot of eggs. So when Lacey gets suspended after tabloid columnist Stella Starbright names him as a "kill-crazy cop," he has to find new work as a private investigator. It's a step down, for sure, and one of his first cases is an unlikely one: former "Stella Starbrights" are turning up dead on the streets of Chicago, and the current one, the reputation ruiner herself, turns to an unlikely source for protection.

Going against his gut, Lacey agrees to keep tabs on Stella to keep her from sharing the grisly fate of her former namesakes. In the midst of all the madness, Lacey hunts the real killer, someone looking to silence gossip columnists for good. But can Lacey crack the case before another victim makes a different section of the newspapers?

Sex…violence…booze! This deadly mix will keep you on the edge of your seat in Ross Spencer's jaded-but-jaunty tale about a hardened cop with nothing but his reputation to lose.

THE DEVEREAUX FILE

Former cop, now private investigator, Lacey Lockington gets lured into a case of something less smooth than his usual tipple: the death of his old drinking buddy and ex-CIA agent Rufe Devereaux. No sooner does he start his investigation than he finds himself chased by the Mafia, hunted by the CIA, stalked by a politician-turned-evangelist out to kill him and "helped" by the sultry Natasha, a KGB agent who always knows more than she lets on. Sucked into the dangerous world of international espionage, Lacey knows he is in way over his head. What started as a search for the truth behind his friend's death turns into a whirlwind tour that leads Lacey from the gritty bars of Chicago to Miami's cocaine-filled underbelly and culminates in an explosive ending that must be read to be believed!

THE FEDOROVICH FILE

The Cold War heats up when trouble comes knocking on the door of ex-cop turned Private Eye Lacey Lockington. Lacey is hot on the trail of Alexi Fedorovich after the high-ranking general publishes a controversial exposé detailing that Glasnost/Perestroika is a hoax. Federovich goes into hiding in the last place he suspects someone will look for him—somewhere in Youngstown, Ohio.

For someone who's pretty much seen and done it all, Lacey's unnerved when he starts dealing with Russian spies, Federal Agents, a man who doesn't want to be found, and an increasing body count of all his leads. Will Lacey, along with former KGB agent and live-in lover Natasha, get to the bottom of it all before Fedorovich finds himself on the wrong end of a firing squad?

Printed in the USA
CPSIA information can be obtained
at www.ICGtesting.com
JSHW031713140824
68134JS00038B/3677